"You wanted to go to bed with me."

"But only on your terms," Sin finished harshly. "And no matter how aroused I may have seemed to you just now, I would never have let it go that far."

"The experience of your added maturity?" Robyn was stung into replying.

"The need for a *real* response from you," he derided bitterly. "If I'd made love to you, you would have been able to console yourself with the notion that I'd seduced you, that you had no choice."

"I have no idea what you're talking about."

"Oh, you know," he contradicted her. "What you want from me is a no-risk affair. But before I've finished with you, you'll be involved right up to your beautiful neck."

Books by Carole Mortimer

HARLEQUIN PRESENTS

These books may be available at your local bookseller.

Don't miss any of our special offers. Write to us at the following address for information on our newest releases.

Harlequin Reader Service
P.O. Box 52040, Phoenix, AZ 85072-2040
Canadian address: P.O. Box 2800, Postal Station A,
5170 Yonge St., Willowdale, Ont. M2N 6J3

CAROLE MORTIMER

a no risk affair

Harlequin Books

TORONTO • NEW YORK • LONDON
AMSTERDAM • PARIS • SYDNEY • HAMBURG
STOCKHOLM • ATHENS • TOKYO • MILAN

For
Joshua John Charles

Harlequin Presents first edition August 1985
ISBN 0-373-10812-5

Original hardcover edition published in 1985
by Mills & Boon Limited

CHAPTER ONE

'HEY, little—er, young lady,' the deeply masculine voice corrected humorously as the man realised his mistake. 'Is your mother at home?'

Robyn had turned slowly to look at the man who had called to her across the garden fence that separated the two cottages, knowing it was this movement that had changed his mind about her being a little girl. From the back her height and slender figure might give that impression, but as soon as she turned that impression was as quickly dispelled. Slender and slightly boyish before the twins were born five years ago her breasts had never returned to their flat-chested state, the clinging blue T-shirt she wore at the moment emphasising that fact.

The man with the wickedly twinkling blue eyes grinned at her devilishly. 'The Colonel told me my new neighbour was a Mrs Warner and her two children, but I had no idea the children would be quite so—grown-up,' his husky voice had lowered appreciatively.

Robyn turned completely now, giving up any idea of hanging up the rest of her washing for the moment, giving him her full attention. 'You're Sinclair Thornton?' her own voice was slightly throaty, almost sensual, not quite in keeping with the fresh-scrubbed look of her face and her long bright red hair secured at her nape.

He leant over the top of the fence, the light summer breeze ruffling his overlong blond hair, his arms deeply tanned below the turned back sleeves of his shirt. 'The Colonel told you about me?' he prompted lightly, giving away nothing of his thoughts on the subject by his bland expression.

She shrugged narrow shoulders. 'There isn't much that's secret in a small community like this one, Mr Thornton,' she answered noncommitally, not willing to admit that she knew his reason for being here, or the fact that she despised that reason utterly.

'My friends call me Sin,' he encouraged softly, his gaze still appreciative.

'So I've heard,' she acknowledged dryly.

Interest flickered in the bright blue eyes. 'What else have you heard?'

'Everyone knows of your books.' Again her manner was slightly reserved. 'They're always on the bestseller list.'

He frowned as he picked up the edge of disapproval in her voice. 'You don't like them?'

'I've never read one,' she told him truthfully. 'I don't have a lot of spare time,' she added by way of softening what could be taken as an insult.

'Of course you don't,' he straightened. 'I'm probably delaying your getting to school right now. I just thought I would introduce myself to your mother.'

Once again he had made the mistake of thinking she was the child instead of the Mrs Warner she actually was, and an imp of devilment stopped her refuting his error. 'I'm the only one at home at the moment,' she said with complete honesty. 'Why don't you come over for dinner this evening?' she invited mischievously. 'I'm sure the rest of the family would love to meet you.' She could well imagine the twins' wide-eyed interest in their new neighbour, and she felt sure this man was going to be more than surprised by who the 'rest of the family' consisted of. It would serve him right for flirting with the impressionable teenager he thought her to be when he was obviously an experienced man in his thirties.

'Are you sure your mother won't mind your making the invitation on her behalf?' he hesitated, obviously not willing to upset his new neighbour on his first day here.

'None of the family will mind,' she told him with certainty, knowing the twins met all too few new people, living on the Masters estate as they did. 'But we eat quite early, about six?' she raised auburn brows enquiringly.

'Anytime suits me,' he accepted. 'I'll look forward to it.'

So would she. It was a long time since she had felt such a mischievous state of anticipation. She hadn't been looking forward to the arrival of her temporary neighbour in the adjoining cottage, knew from his reputation and the life he had led that he would be too much like Brad for comfort. In looks the two men were opposite, Brad as dark as Sinclair Thornton was blond, Brad's eyes a cold calculating grey whereas the other man's were a bright twinkling blue. But Sinclair Thornton had once been a reporter, as Brad still was, and although the other man appeared to have had the sense to get out while he was still in one piece, both emotionally and physically, Brad still went to all the trouble spots of the world, throwing himself into the task with a relish that sickened her. Although she and her ex-husband had been divorced for almost two years he still popped up from time to time, showered gifts on Kim and Andy when they would much rather have had more of his time and love, before disappearing off to God knows where again.

It had been the constant uncertainty as to Brad's welfare, the days, weeks sometimes, of waiting to see if he would get out of his latest assignment alive, that had completed the erosion of their marriage. And she knew, as did most other people, that the bestselling books that Sinclair Thornton specialised in were for the main part based on his own experiences during his time as a reporter, that 'only the names and places had been changed to protect the innocent'! And from the reviews she had read of those books there didn't appear to be many of the latter between the covers!

When the Colonel had told her of the author's proposed visit here she had been less than enthusiastic, despised the glorifying of war when it *was* the innocent who suffered. And as Sinclair Thornton had made it known that he intended basing his next book, in part, on the Colonel's war-time experiences she couldn't say she had relished the thought of meeting him.

But he had turned out to be slightly different from what she had imagined, although she didn't doubt that the same hardness that had ruled all Brad's decisions in life lurked somewhere beneath the easygoing charm of the other man; no man could see and experience some of the things those two had without becoming hardened to the softer things in life such as love and children.

But this thinking of Sinclair Thornton wouldn't do, she had to be up at the Hall for nine-fifteen, and she still had a few things to do before then. 'We'll see you at six, then, Mr Thornton,' she told him dismissively.

'Yes,' but he made no effort to move. 'Er—Do you think I might borrow a cup of milk? I only arrived an hour ago and I'm afraid milk isn't something I thought to buy.'

She almost laughed out loud at the little-boy-lost-look he had suddenly affected. 'So much for wanting to introduce yourself,' she mocked as she turned to go into her own little cottage.

'But I did,' Sinclair Thornton had moved with lightning speed through the gate that connected the two gardens and was now walking at her side with long, easy strides, his denims old and faded as they rested low down on his hips, his black shirt fitted over his wide shoulders and tapered waist.

She looked up at him with mocking eyes, barely reaching his shoulder, made to feel like the little girl he had first presumed her to be. 'You just thought that as I was here...' she drawled teasingly.

'Exactly,' he grinned, his eyes crinkling as laughter lines fanned out from the corners, a dimple appearing in one of his lean cheeks. 'See, I didn't even bring a cup with me,' he held up his empty hands.

They were nice hands, strong and capable looking, the fingers long and fleshless, in fact the whole of his body didn't possess an ounce of superfluous weight. He certainly hadn't let his fame and fortune soften him! It was another reminder for her—if she needed one!—that his charm and easygoing manner were only skin-deep too.

'I'm sure I can manage to let you keep the cup until this evening,' her voice had hardened.

'I promise I'll bring it back,' he nodded, looking about the kitchen appreciatively, obviously liking the yellow and white decor in the tiny room, his gaze coming to rest on the obviously childish paintings she had pinned to the walls. 'Your brother or sister must be a lot younger than you?' he raised blond brows questioningly.

'Andy is only five,' she acknowledged noncommittally, handing him the cup of milk, her expectant stare clearly saying she wanted him to leave now.

'I'm looking forward to a home-cooked meal,' he told her by way of parting.

'Don't look forward to it too much,' Robyn warned with a grin. 'I—My mother isn't the best cook in the world.'

'After some of my own efforts in that direction anything will taste good,' he assured her, not seeming to have noticed her slip.

He had disappeared into the adjoining cottage by the time she returned to the garden to finish hanging out the washing. Which was perhaps as well, because she had got to the twins clothes now, the numerous trousers, T-shirts and skirts obviously for more than one child. Sinclair Thornton would only have to glance over this way once some time during the day and he would realise the mistake he had made. Would he be amused or annoyed that she hadn't corrected him?

Oh well, it had only been a harmless joke. And if he was going to be their neighbour for the next few months he would have to learn to cope with that sort of thing, both Kim and Andy having inherited their mother's sense of fun.

Now that the early morning rush was over, the twins washed and dressed, their breakfasts cooked and eaten, and the two of them safely on board the bus that would take them to the school three miles away, she had time to get herself ready for work.

The denims and T-shirt were the first to go, replaced with one of the tailored skirts and a tan blouse she had bought herself for work. Then came her make-up, the shadings subdued, her lipgloss a deep plum colour, her cheeks lightly highlighted with blusher. And lastly came her hair. Released from the ribbon at her nape it flowed in a glorious red cascade down her back. But she didn't leave it in that style, knew that the loose coil on top of her head added to her maturity if it didn't help her look her twenty-four years.

Twenty-four, was that really all she was? Sometimes she felt twice that age, and at other times she wondered where all the years had gone to, the time seeming to have flown by since the twins were born. Married at eighteen, a mother—and more or less a grass-widow—at nineteen, divorced at only twenty-two, a lot had happened to her in the last six years. If she hadn't had the twins she didn't know how she would have coped with half of it. It was ironic, in the circumstances, that the two babies she loved more than anything else in the world had also been partly responsible, innocently, for most of what had happened after they were born. Although perhaps that wasn't quite true, it had been Brad's reaction to them that had been the cause of that.

She walked the mile and a half up to Bromptwood Hall, leaving her little car and the petrol she guarded so frugally, in the garage next to the cottage. She enjoyed the walk anyway, and she preferred to use what petrol she could afford to buy to take Kim and Andy out at the weekends. All three of them looked forward to and enjoyed these trips, and on warm days like this one her walk to work became a pleasure. She would think about the cold days when they arrived!

The office she occupied during the morning was next to the Colonel's study, the post already on her desk to be sorted and dealt with before lunch. In the afternoon she would become one of the guides for the tours around the historic house and gardens, enjoying that part of her work most of all, liking to talk to the people who visited, finding pleasure in showing them the grand old house.

Colonel Masters had married the daughter of the house, an only child, twenty-five years ago, and when his wife died eight years ago and the estate became expensive to run he had decided to open his doors to the public during the summer months, as a lot of other stately homes had been pressured into doing in recent years. It certainly didn't make him a fortune, but it kept him and his daughter Caroline in relative comfort, had also helped to send the latter to the exclusive school in Switzerland she had returned from only this summer.

If there were a black spot on Robyn's horizon it was the other girl. Spoilt and pampered all her life Caroline looked down on anyone who had to work for a living, treating most of the estate staff as inferior to herself, Robyn more so than most. She considered Robyn had been highly stupid to have got herself married and divorced to a man who hadn't even been able to give her a decent allowance after the divorce.

The younger girl sauntered into Robyn's office halfway through the morning, her dress made exclusively for her in London, her dark beauty emphasised by the delicate shade of blue. A deep admirer of the Princess of Wales—as were most women!—Caroline made it her business to have her clothes designed by the same people the Princess did. The fact that she was shorter and plumper than the Princess escaped her, as did the fact that she could never look quite as elegant as that famous lady, no matter what clothes she wore.

'Daddy wants you to work late today,' she told Robyn in a bored voice.

She heaved an inward sigh, knowing she was in for an argument. 'The Colonel knows very well that I can't do that.' She always finished promptly at three-fifteen so that she could be home in time to meet the twins off the school bus.

'Because of those two brats of yours, I suppose,' Caroline derided. 'Can't they let themselves into the cottage for once?'

Dark brown eyes clashed with a callous blue. 'No,' Robyn replied emphatically.

'Well, can't you get someone to sit with them until you get home?' the younger girl was showing her impatience now.

Robyn eyed her with suspicion. 'Why does your father want me to work late?'

Caroline shrugged. 'There's a late party

coming at three-thirty, and as you know it's Maggie's day off . . .'

She also knew that on the rare occasions that this happened the Colonel made alternative arrangements, ones that didn't include her working late; he had even taken the odd party around himself when necessary. The Colonel may not be the easiest man in the world to get on with but he did understand her home situation. 'Your father told me he was going to ask you to take that party,' she challenged.

Caroline's pretty face flushed her displeasure. 'I have a hair appointment this afternoon.'

Robyn looked at the already perfectly styled dark hair. 'You look just fine to me,' she dismissed.

The younger girl gave her a scathing look. 'And we all know how qualified you are to judge!'

She knew the other girl considered her casual clothes, light make-up, and unfashionably long hair excluded her from being able to talk with any authority on all three of them. And maybe they did, but she always knew what was in fashion nowadays—she only had to look at Caroline for that. It was strange really, there were only four years difference in their ages, and yet she felt so much older than the other girl, had found much more important things than fashion to fill and enrich her life.

'Take your choice, Caroline,' she shrugged. 'Go down to the cottage and sit with the twins or take the party round.' Her expression was widely innocent as she saw the other girl's look of horror at the mention of the twins.

'Those little devils!' Caroline gasped.

'They love you too, Caroline,' she drawled,

knowing the dislike was mutual. Her exuberant offspring couldn't understand why Caroline refused to get down on the floor with them or go out in the garden and play in the dirt, pursuits their mother didn't seem to mind in the least. In fact, Robyn rather enjoyed playing with her children.

Irritation darkened the hard blue eyes. 'The last time I called Kim laddered my tights by crawling all over me and Andy spilt orange juice all over my new dress.'

'Both incidents were accidents,' she defended, knowing that her children didn't have a vindictive bone in their bodies. 'And it was only one little spot of orange juice, it sponged off quite easily.'

'Luckily for you,' Caroline snapped waspishly. 'You don't exactly earn enough here to have replaced the dress, and I doubt Brad remembers to send your maintenance any more often than he used to.'

She flushed her resentment at the personal remark, knowing it was inevitable that people should be aware of her private business in the rural community that she had chosen to live in, also knowing that Caroline wasn't averse to using her knowledge when she felt like being particularly bitchy. 'We manage,' she bit out tautly.

Caroline smiled her pleasure at being able to pierce the shield of calmness that so irritated her. 'My dear cousin never was a reliable husband,' she mocked. 'Was he?' she taunted.

It wasn't difficult to imagine Brad and Caroline as being closely related. Brad may hide his selfish preoccupation with his own needs better than Caroline did, but the trait was there nonetheless. Brad was the son of the Colonel's

sister, and it was the Colonel who had offered her
and the twins the use of one of the estate cottages
when she and Brad had first separated, claiming
that family should stick together no matter what,
that there had never been a divorce in the family.
And for a while Brad had visited the three of
them at the cottage, before even that trailed off.
But the Colonel had insisted she and the twins
stay on at the estate, had even given her the job as
his own secretary. Not that she had ever felt part
of the Masters family, but the job and cottage
were very welcome, especially when, as Caroline
pointed out so maliciously, Brad was so remiss
with monetary support for his children. For
herself she didn't care, but for the twins she
minded a great deal.

Not that any of that showed in her face as she
looked up at Caroline. 'He sends what he can
when he can,' she murmured stiffly.

'Are you kidding?' the younger girl scoffed.
'He must earn a small fortune doing the job he
does, and you don't see a penny of it!'

'Caroline——'

'*I* wouldn't let him get away with it,' she
declared haughtily. 'Although how the two of you
ever got married in the first place I'll never
know!' she added scornfully.

Robyn had often wondered about that herself
since the separation and divorce, had come to the
conclusion that it was her near hero-worship of
Brad that had persuaded him to marry her. At the
time she had been too much in love with him to
realise how ill-suited they were. She had been
eighteen to his twenty-eight, had found Brad
exciting just to be with, had been wide-eyed and
innocent about physical relationships, not having

had a lover before Brad. The proof of that innocence had been her pregnancy only two months after their wedding! Brad had been furious at her stupidity, had taken it for granted that she would be responsible for any use of contraception between them. The rage he had flown into when he learnt he was to be a father had been only the first of many.

'I don't believe this is any of your business, Caroline,' she said distantly.

'Maybe not,' the younger girl shrugged. 'But cousin-by-marriage or not, I am not looking after your two brats this afternoon.'

'Kim and Andy are not brats——'

'They're always into one scrape or another——'

'That's just high spirits!'

'Was it "high spirits" when they knocked over the Christmas tree last year?'

Robyn sighed. 'It was an accident. Kim slipped on one of the rugs in the hall.' And she could still remember her horror as the huge decorated tree had crashed down on her tiny daughter.

'It was a mess,' Caroline remembered disgustedly.

'Maybe when you've given your father grandchildren of his own he'll stop feeling compelled to invite us to join your festivities,' she derided.

'I don't intend ruining my figure giving some man children he'll probably ignore.'

Robyn ignored this latest jibe at Brad and herself. 'It improved mine,' she smiled.

'Maybe on the surface,' Caroline acknowledged. 'But stretch marks can be so unsightly!'

Robyn didn't even attempt to defend this insult. She had a few finely silver stretch marks on the flatness of her abdomen, yes, but unless someone was looking really closely they weren't noticeable. And she knew that she would risk having much worse marks than that if she could have Kim and Andy at the end of it. 'So you'll be taking the party around this afternoon?' she said dryly.

Caroline flashed her an angry look. 'If you weren't family you wouldn't be so sure of yourself,' she snapped.

If she didn't at least have that claim she didn't know if she would be able to stand Caroline's constant bitchiness. At least this way she was partly able to defend herself, although at the back of her mind she always had the danger of losing her home and job. Caroline did have a lot of influence with her over-indulgent father, and if she made enough of a fuss about Robyn and her children he could just be talked into asking them to leave. Nevertheless, she never let herself or the twins be treated as inferiors; there were some limits to her pride.

'If I weren't family then I wouldn't be here,' she pointed out in a reasoning tone. 'And couldn't you have your hair done tomorrow?'

'I wanted to look good for when Sinclair Thornton arrives,' her cousin-by-marriage said moodily.

'He's arrived.'

Blue eyes sharpened questioningly. 'What do you mean?'

She shrugged narrow shoulders. 'Exactly what I said, he's already arrived.'

'When?'

'This morning.'

'You've seen him?'

Robyn nodded. 'Before I came to work. Your father didn't mention his arrival to you?'

'No,' she answered in a preoccupied voice. 'But then he's been rather busy this morning.' Caroline's expression was sharp as she focused on Robyn. 'What's he like?'

'Mr Thornton?'

'Well I hardly mean Daddy!'

She had known exactly who Caroline meant, but the occasional need to bait the younger girl persisted. The two of them had never got on, Caroline seeming to have more poise and sophistication even at fourteen than the young girl being introduced as the newest member of the family. It soon became obvious that even this youngest member of the family found her unsophisticated naïveté totally unsuitable in a relation of hers. And just occasionally Robyn couldn't help the defence mechanism that sprang into action whenever she remembered those past slights, motherhood having given her a confidence she previously lacked. Finding herself solely responsible at nineteen for two other vulnerable lives besides her own was sure to have had some effect!

'Mr Thornton seemed—quite pleasant,' she answered dismissively.

'As good looking at his photographs?' Caroline couldn't keep the eagerness out of her voice as she forgot for a moment her usual affected air of boredom.

Sinclair Thornton's good looks couldn't be denied, neither could his charm, and yet somehow she doubted he was exactly Caroline's type. The men the younger girl usually dated all seemed to be highly sophisticated, always per-

fectly dressed for the occasion, and Robyn felt
sure that any denims those men owned would
carry designer labels on the back and not be as
disreputably faded and old as the denims Sinclair
Thornton had worn this morning had been. But
maybe she was misjudging Caroline, maybe the
author's raw masculinity would be a welcome
change after all that polished charm.

'I've never seen a photograph of him,' she
shrugged. 'But he is very good looking.'

Caroline chewed thoughtfully on her bottom
lip, seemingly unaware that she was smudging
her lipgloss by doing so, something she wouldn't
be pleased about when she realised it later. 'I
wonder if it would be too forward of me to go
over and introduce myself?' she murmured to
herself.

Remembering the author's casually friendly
manner Robyn doubted he would find it at all
forward to have a beautiful young girl introduce
herself to him. 'I'm sure he would welcome it,'
she drawled.

Caroline looked at her with narrowed blue
eyes. 'I don't want to go down there if you've
already made a nuisance of yourself,' she
questioned haughtily.

Robyn held on to her temper with effort. One
of these days——! She didn't have red hair for
nothing, as Caroline would one day find out if
she didn't stop playing 'Lady of the Manor' in
this way! 'I didn't make a nuisance of myself at
all, he came over to borrow a cup of milk——'

'How original!'

'You said it,' she sighed wearily.

Caroline flushed at her misdirected sarcasm.
'I'm sure he really did need the milk.'

'So am I,' she said dryly. 'An author would be able to think of a much better approach.'

'Of course,' the younger girl scorned. 'I think I'll go and invite him over to dinner tonight, I'm sure he can't be organised enough for that yet.'

'Er . . .'

'Yes?' Caroline prompted impatiently.

She gave a resigned sigh. 'He's coming to the cottage for dinner this evening,' she revealed reluctantly.

'The cottage?' the other girl repeated dumbfoundedly. 'You mean with you and the twins?'

'Well as we're the ones that live there, yes,' she nodded.

Caroline flushed at the sarcasm. 'What on earth possessed you to invite a man like Sinclair Thornton to dinner?' she snapped disgustedly.

'What on earth possessed *him* to accept?' she flashed back, her eyes dark.

'Politeness, I expect,' Caroline returned waspishly, her eyes suddenly narrowing again. 'You aren't seriously interested in him, are you?' she said disbelievingly.

Robyn flushed at the younger girl's incredulity at such an idea being possible. The fact that she never dated, that a man like Sinclair Thornton would be the last man she would be attracted to if she did, didn't alter the fact that Caroline seemed to think she had no right to find any member of the opposite sex attractive, that her divorce and motherhood meant she had to be unattractive herself to any man.

'I was merely being a polite neighbour,' she bit out tightly. 'If he would rather accept your invitation then I won't be in the least insulted.' Any imp of pleasure she may have got out of this

morning's teasing of Sinclair Thornton had
evaporated during this unpleasant exchange with
Caroline. It probably wouldn't have been funny
anyway, not if Sinclair Thornton felt about
children the same way Caroline did.

'I should hope not,' Caroline said haughtily.
'The man is here to see Daddy, after all.'

'Yes.'

'I'll just go and change before going down
there,' Caroline spoke softly to herself, her smile
one of anticipation.

'Er—Caroline?' she halted the other girl at the
door. 'The coach-party this afternoon?' she
prompted, having received no definite reply on
the matter.

The pouting red mouth tightened. 'I'll have to
take them round, I expect,' she snapped.
'Daddy's silly to be so soft with you, you are an
employee, after all.'

Robyn made no reply to this last bitchiness,
although her breath left her in a barely controlled
sigh once she was alone. It was true, she was an
employee, but the Colonel always made allowances
for the fact that she was a single parent first. She
had no doubt that if, or when, anything happened
to the Colonel there would be a lot of changes made.

She had never thought of herself as totally
ineligible before, either. Oh the twins would be a
big responsibility for any man to take on if he
should happen to fall in love with her, but she
had never even thought of being on her own for
the rest of her life, knew that although she had
had one disastrous marriage that with another
man it could all be perfect. For the moment she
preferred things the way they were, knew that
although Kim and Andy were well-adjusted

children that the fact that their father had chosen
not to live with them troubled them at times. But
one day they would be old enough to understand,
and when that day came she would be ready
herself to perhaps find a new love of her own.
For the moment she was satisfied with her lot.

And for Caroline to imply she might be
interested in Sinclair Thornton was ridiculous!
He wasn't her type at all, and she doubted she
was his either.

The twins were particularly boisterous when they
got home that evening, and it took a good play
and their baths to calm them down enough for
their evening meal. Not that Robyn had gone to
any trouble over the latter, fully expecting that
Caroline would be able to convince Sinclair
Thornton that dinner at the Hall would be much
more comfortable. Not that Caroline had come to
tell her of the change of plans, she hadn't seen the
other girl all afternoon, but she took it for
granted that she and the twins would be eating
alone as usual. And if their neighbour did
happen, by some remote chance, to come to them
for dinner there was enough casserole for all of
them. It may not be what he was used to, or what
he would have got at the Hall, but it was good
food, and well cooked.

'Is Daddy coming to see us this weekend?'
Andy asked as she helped the two of them to
dress upstairs after their bath, as alike as two peas
to look at, both having Robyn's bright red hair
and warm brown eyes.

'Not this weekend,' she dismissed lightly,
brushing her daughter's unruly curls into some
order before they dried.

'It's ages since he came,' Andy said moodily.

'He's busy,' his sister put in quietly, the younger by five minutes, also the more introvert of the two; Kim tended to follow where Andy led, her brother outspoken as well as outgoing.

'Yes. But——'

'Kim's right, Andy,' Robyn told him brightly. 'Daddy has to work very hard. And it's only a few weeks since he telephoned you both.' For a total of five minutes, she thought bitterly. Not once had she tried to deter Brad from seeing the children, or to influence them in any way concerning his long absences, it had all been Brad's decision, although she couldn't help the inner resentment she felt on the twins' behalf at his lack of interest in them, knew that Kim was as hurt by it as Andy, no matter how much she defended him. Sometimes, when she felt her children's pain the most, she wished Brad would just stay out of their lives completely, let the twins forget him. But life just wasn't that tidy or straightforward. And maybe it was a selfish wish, the twins loved their father however little they saw of him, and perhaps in his own way he loved them too.

She was stopped from making further comment by the ringing of the doorbell, a glance at her watch as Andy leapt to look out of the window showing her it was exactly six o'clock!

'There's a man outside, Mummy,' Andy told her excitedly.

She stood up slowly, feeling a moment's panic before she instantly calmed again. Probably Sinclair Thornton had come to apologetically explain that he was going up to the Hall for dinner. Yes, that would be it. 'Finish getting dressed, children,' she told them in a preoccupied voice. 'I—I'll go and see who it is.' She hadn't mentioned the possibility of a guest for dinner to them, they were too often let down by their father without a complete stranger doing it too!

She checked her appearance in the mirror in the hallway before going to the door. If anything she looked even younger than she had this morning! She released her hair about her shoulders, wishing she had time to change from the cut-off denims and cream sun-top. But the doorbell ringing for a second time made that impossible.

As she had guessed, her caller was Sinclair Thornton, a bunch of tulips in one hand as his eyes gleamed at her mischievously over the petals. He wore fitted brown trousers and a lemon shirt tonight, but he looked no less ruggedly attractive in this slightly more formal clothing.

'Hi,' he greeted softly. 'I'm not too early, am I?' he added as she made no move to let him in.

'Er—no,' she blinked her surprise. 'It's just—Caroline—Miss Masters, said something about inviting you up to the Hall tonight.'

'She did,' he nodded. 'But I had to refuse her, after all I had already accepted your invitation.'

'Oh but——' She was stopped from further speech by the clatter of small feet down the stairs behind her, turning to see the twins arrive at the bottom together, looking adorably innocent with their newly washed faces and hair, wearing identical blue T-shirts and denims.

Robyn turned back to apologise to their guest for keeping him on the doorstep, her eyes widening as she saw his stunned expression, his incredulity obvious as he stared at the twins. Whatever he and Caroline had discussed after he had refused the other girl's invitation this afternoon he certainly hadn't been told of the twins' existence!

CHAPTER TWO

'PLEASE, come in,' she huskily invited the still silent Sinclair Thornton, relieved when he did so, taking him into her small but comfortable lounge. The twins stared back at him, as wide-eyed as he was, and she put a protective hand on either of their shoulders as she looked at Sinclair Thornton with challenging eyes. 'I don't think we introduced ourselves properly this morning,' she told him softly. 'I am Robyn Warner, and these are my two children, Kim and Andy.'

Considering how shocked he had been seconds earlier he was recovering well, the gleam back in his blue eyes as he began to smile. 'I'm sure it was just an oversight on your part,' he drawled mockingly. 'And in that case, these are for you.' He held out the tulips for her. 'I'm afraid I forgot the cup, *Mrs* Warner,' he added pointedly.

'My friends call me Robyn,' she returned much as he had done this morning.

'Can I?' he teased.

'Please,' she nodded, relieved that he had taken her deception so well.

'Well, Kim and Andy, you just have to be twins,' he spoke to them in a pleasantly interested voice, and not down to them as so many adults tended to do. 'And both as cute as your mother,' he teased.

Andy giggled at this description being given to his mother. 'Mummy isn't cute,' he scorned. 'She's beautiful.'

Appreciative blue eyes swept over her blushing face. 'So she is,' Sinclair Thornton said slowly.

'I'll just go and put these in water,' Robyn said awkwardly, instantly annoyed with herself for appearing so gauche. No doubt Caroline would have accepted the compliment with much more aplomb! But then, the younger girl was used to the meaningless charm, she wasn't. 'Perhaps the children would like to show you some of their toys while I'm gone,' she added briskly.

It took her only a few minutes to put the tulips in water and check that the dinner was ready, stopping in the lounge doorway when she got back. She should have known Sinclair Thornton was one of those men who found children's toys as fascinating as they did! He was down on the floor with Kim and Andy, with little regard for his clothes, seemingly fascinated by the workings of the dolls' house and fort the two of them had received recently for their fifth birthdays.

He looked up sheepishly as he sensed Robyn watching him. 'I never can resist these things.' He put one of the soldiers up on the battlements.

She smiled, sure that all men were still children at heart. 'Do you have children of your own, Mr Thornton?'

'Not at the moment, no,' he shook his head. 'And it's Sin,' he reminded.

She knew what his name was, she just felt uncomfortable saying it, the name Sin making *her* feel wicked too! And what did 'not at the moment' mean? Was he, like Brad, a part-time father who chose to forget about his children when he wasn't actually with them, or did he mean he was contemplating fatherhood? Maybe what she should have asked him was whether or not he was married.

'Sin was once a reporter like Daddy,' Kim put in eagerly, obviously considering that anyone who was remotely like her father was okay by her.

'I know,' she replied stiffly, amazed that had been revealed in the short time she had been in the kitchen. 'Can you put some of those things away while I serve dinner?' They had managed to get out an awful lot of toys during her absence too!

'Did you lose your husband very long ago?'

Robyn almost dropped the vegetable bowl she had carefully been pouring peas into at the sound of that husky voice just behind her, having been unaware of the fact that Sinclair Thornton had followed her.

'Careful.' Sin took the bowl out of her hands. 'The twins have gone to wash their hands for dinner so I thought I would join you. I didn't mean to startle you.'

'You didn't,' she assured him stiltedly.

'Then my question did,' he said shrewdly, watching her with narrowed eyes. 'Which means it must have been recently. I'm sorry, I——'

'I wouldn't call four years ago recently, Mr Thornton,' she dismissed briskly. 'Now shall we go in to dinner before everything gets cold?'

She was slightly ashamed of her waspish behaviour as he did everything he could through the meal to be interesting and interested in her children, effectively covering up any prolonged silence on her part. He had caught her offguard with his question about Brad; having lived in Colton for so long she wasn't used to having to explain her single-parent state to anyone, everyone already *knew*! But of course this man couldn't be expected to know anything about her past life, and after the trick she had played on him this morning he was entitled to be curious.

He didn't even attempt to interfere in her nightly ritual of putting the twins to bed, as some other over-eager adults had done in the past, and because he didn't Kim and Andy made the request for him to go up to their bedroom and say good night to them, an honour few were granted.

'You're very good with children,' Robyn turned to smile at him as they returned to the lounge.

He shrugged his broad shoulders. 'I try to be.'

That was the whole point, he didn't 'try' at all, and the children loved him for it. 'Coffee?' she offered.

'Let me make it.' He followed her through to the kitchen, the four of them having already done the washing-up, a hilarious affair, with Sin pretending to drop things. 'You sit down and rest for a few minutes, you must have had a long day.'

Robyn sat as he deftly prepared the coffee. It was nice to be waited on for a change.

'That was a stupid thing for me to have said,' Sin realised as he poured their coffee. 'Every day must be a long one for you.'

'A six-thirty start can be a bit tiring,' she admitted. 'But it has its compensations.'

He nodded. 'I'm sure it does. I'm sorry about earlier,' he added gently. 'I didn't mean to pry.'

'You didn't,' she shrugged, carrying the tray through to the lounge. 'It was just natural curiosity.'

'Hm,' he grimaced acknowledgment. 'And I seem to have rather a lot of that.'

'Surely that's only natural in your profession?'
She sat across the room from him.

'Some people don't like it.' He leant back in his
chair, totally relaxed, having eaten the casserole
with relish, and having had two helpings of apple
pie, much to the twins' delight. 'It's a bit like
being a doctor or a psychiatrist, people don't
altogether trust your motives for talking to them,
think you're analysing them, in my case for a
character in one of my books,' he revealed dryly.

She smiled. 'And don't you?'

He grinned, the devilish twinkle back in his
deep blue eyes. 'I suppose I do, sometimes. But it
isn't done consciously,' he defended.

'I'm sure most people consider it a compliment
to recognise themselves in one of your books.'

'That's the problem,' his humour deepened.
'Most people don't see themselves in the character
I create for them, see themselves entirely
different to the way I do. Several of them have
threatened to sue in the past.'

'Oh dear,' she laughed. 'Then let's hope the
Colonel isn't one of them!'

'You know my reason for being here?' he
seemed surprised.

'I'm the Colonel's secretary,' she explained.

'You're RDW,' he realised in amazement,
referring to her initials that always appeared at
the top of the letters he had received from the
Colonel during their negotiations for him to come
here and interview the older man.

'It's a small place,' she shrugged.

'I know,' he nodded. 'I took a look around this
afternoon, talked to a few of the locals. The
Colonel seems to be a well-liked man.'

'I'm sure he is,' she replied noncommittally,

unwilling to discuss anything concerning her employer.

'What happened to your husband?' Sin suddenly asked in the silence of the room.

Robyn blinked her surprise. 'Are you always this—forthright?'

'My reporter's instincts,' he apologised.

'Of course,' she realised dryly. 'For a moment I forgot . . .' She sighed. 'Nothing "happened" to my husband.'

'You mean he just died?'

'Died?' she repeated incredulously.

'Well he obviously isn't here now, and the Colonel told me you live here alone with your children . . .'

'I see,' she frowned. 'He isn't dead either. Brad is still very much alive.'

'Brad?' Sin repeated slowly. 'Are you saying *Brad* Warner is your husband?'

She flushed at his incredulity, knowing herself now what an unlikely combination they must seem. 'Ex-husband,' she confirmed abruptly. 'We're divorced.'

'I didn't even know he was married,' Sin seemed stunned by the revelation. 'Let alone that he had two children too.'

Her mouth twisted. 'It isn't something he likes to broadcast,' she drawled.

Sin looked disconcerted by what she had just told him. 'You must have been very young when you and he got married.'

She shrugged. 'Age can be used as an excuse for many mistakes. And no, the twins were not conceived until after the wedding,' she added dryly, knowing that was the next question that would occur to most people.

'But surely——'

'I don't like to talk about my marriage—Sin,' she at last managed to say his name, wondering if other women felt as she did when they said it, a thrill of wicked delight shivering down her spine. 'It was all in the past, and life has to go on.'

'Even that seems too cynical coming from such a young and beautiful woman,' he frowned.

He wasn't flirting with her, she could tell that, he genuinely found it disconcerting that she should have found such cynicism in her life at such a young age. 'Do I seem bitter to you?' she cajoled.

'No,' he acknowledged.

'And you find that surprising,' she realised.

'A little,' he nodded. 'I've known Brad on a casual basis for over ten years, and he never spoke of a wife and children. We've never been bosom buddies or anything, there isn't time for that in reporting, but even so most men talk about their wife and families at some time.'

'Brad is totally dedicated to his job,' she dismissed without emotion.

'So was I once, but——'

'What made you make the change from reporting to writing novels?' she cut in interestedly.

He looked at her for several minutes, her own gaze unflinching. 'You want to change the subject?' he grimaced ruefully.

'I think it might be a good idea,' she said without rancour. She knew his interest in her marriage was mainly caused by the fact that he was surprised at who her husband had been more than a real need to pry. It hadn't occurred to her that Sin and Brad would know each other, although she had always known that the world of the press was a pretty closed one, so much so that even the spouses lost out to it.

'It's a small world, isn't it?' Sin obviously echoed some of her thoughts.

'Sometimes it would seem to be,' she agreed softly.

'Do you ever see him now?'

She didn't pretend to misunderstand. 'He comes down to see the twins.'

Sin shook his head. 'I'm prying again,' he apologised. 'And I've also forgotten what you asked me.'

She smiled her sympathy with his confusion. 'Why you became a writer instead of a reporter.'

'It seemed a natural progression from what I was doing,' he shrugged. 'The type of reporting I was involved in is for the young; I would have been given a permanent desk job eventually, anyway.'

'You make it sound as if you're ancient,' she teased.

'Thirty-seven,' he supplied. 'I made the decison to get out of the rat-race five years ago.'

And it had obviously been a wise decision. She would have put him at much younger than his years, younger than Brad when he was actually three years the other man's senior. 'It's obviously been a successful decision,' she said noncommittally.

'Luckily,' he nodded. 'I could quite easily have disappeared into obscurity along with a million other would-be-writers. I never forget to be grateful I'm one of the lucky few who made it.'

'Surely your success is due to a lot more than just luck,' she chided.

'Maybe you're right, if I couldn't write the public wouldn't still be buying my books. But at the same time a lot of it depends on whether your style of book is in fashion when you start out; tastes change all the time.'

'I suppose so,' she agreed. 'And never having read one myself I have no idea whether you're talented or just lucky,' she teased. But she did know, knew that he would be extremely talented, that this man, with his quiet air of confidence, would be good at whatever he chose to do.

'Shame on you,' he grinned, the mood of seriousness forgotten. 'Even my mother has read one or two of them, and she isn't interested in anything but gardening!'

Robyn's mouth twisted. 'I'm sure she's interested in her son.'

His smile deepened. 'I'm sure she is too,' he acknowledged ruefully. 'And all this time I thought she actually liked my books,' he added self-derisively.

'Do you have any other family?' she asked interestedly.

'A father and an older brother,' he nodded, the blue eyes twinkling merrily as her eyes widened at the latter. 'Don't I come over as the baby of the family?' he mocked.

He 'came over' as a man so sure of himself and his own capabilities that he had no need of the charm he had also been endowed with, although he could also use that to great advantage when he chose to. The twins had been fascinated by him, and not just because he had once done the same job as their Daddy. They had even solicited a promise from him that he would take them swimming some time. Kim and Andy loved to go to the pool at the Hall, but as the invitations to use the small indoor pool there, understandably with Caroline's aversion to them, weren't too plentiful, they had to make the trip into town to the public pool if they wanted to swim. Robyn knew that the twins' desire to spend more time with Sin Thornton didn't come just from the fact that their own trips to the pool were governed by finances; that they genuinely liked the man.

And she wasn't so sure that was a good thing. With the lack of a permanent father figure in their life the twins were apt to find the company of any available male something to be prized above everything else. Sin Thornton could just find himself in the role of surrogate father for the time he was here.

'Not particularly,' she answered his question in a preoccupied voice. 'What does your father do?'

'Now? Nothing,' he shook his head. 'He's a retired newspaperman.'

'I didn't think they did retire,' her voice had sharpened perceptively. 'I thought they just got old—or killed.'

'Robyn——' he broke off as the forlorn voice of her daughter called down to them, frowning his concern at the sound.

'Don't worry,' Robyn dismissed lightly, rising slowly to her feet. 'This is a nightly ritual,' she mocked. 'I even know to take the glasses of water upstairs with me now to save myself a second trip.'

'Oh, I see,' Sin grinned.

'One of these days they're going to realise that I've caught on to their little game,' she drawled. 'I shouldn't be long,' she added before leaving the room.

'Don't hurry on my account,' he called after her softly. 'I'm perfectly comfortable.'

She was aware of that. In fact, he was slumped so comfortably in the chair she was beginning to wonder if he were ever going to leave. And she wanted him to. Already he had touched on subjects she would rather not discuss. If he didn't leave soon who knew what outrage he would come out with?

The twins looked adorable in their adjoining twin beds, and she pushed aside the worrying thought of what she was going to do when they became old enough to require separate bedrooms. They would work that problem out when they came to it, as they had many others the last five years, and although it might not be the ideal solution Kim could always move in with her when the time came.

She handed them each the wanted glass of water, sitting down on the edge of Kim's bed as they sat up to drink. The demand for a drink of water soon after they were in bed had started about six months ago, and although she didn't really like to encourage such tactics for attention, she knew that Kim and Andy would settle down to sleep within ten minutes of her leaving the room with the empty glasses. Maybe they really did want the water, or maybe like her, they just enjoyed the little chats they had as she waited for the glasses to empty. Whatever the reason she herself enjoyed these few minutes of quiet calm with her offspring at the end of a long day.

'Is Sin still downstairs?' the more forthright of her children asked eagerly.

Robyn gave him an indulgent smile. 'Yes.'

'He's nice,' Kim put in shyly, her long hair

secured neatly at her nape with a brown ribbon.

'Yes, he is,' she agreed noncommittally. 'Now what would the two of you like to do this weekend?' The mention of their weekend outings was sure to divert their attention from their new neighbour.

'Maybe we could all go swimming?' Kim suggested eagerly.

Robyn had realised her mistake in mentioning going out on Saturday the moment identical brown eyes lit up excitedly. Too late she realised it. But she had no wish to spend any more time with Sinclair Thornton than she had to; being neighbourly was one thing, anything more than that she wasn't interested in. He was a pleasant enough man, a handsome one, she couldn't deny that, but she had enough problems already without causing the unnecessary jealousy of Caroline Masters. Caroline was going to be angry enough about Sin choosing to come here this evening without that! Robyn had no doubt she would have to suffer the sharp edge of the younger woman's tongue because of it.

'I don't think so, Kim,' she smiled to take the disappointment out of her words. 'Mr Thornton is here to work, not to amuse us.'

'But he said——'

'You asked him, Andy,' she reprimanded her son gently. 'The poor man had no choice but to say yes.'

The freckled face beneath her looked rebellious, and despite looking like her in every way Robyn could see Brad in her son in that moment. The wilful single-mindedness Andy occasionally displayed worried her at times, she had to admit that, and she was aware of the fact that he could become as unmanageable and unreasonable as his father when he was older if he didn't have the right handling now. But no one had ever told her that being a parent was easy, and if she occasionally wished she had someone she could rely on and ask for advice the feeling quickly passed. Brad had never given any indication that he regretted their divorce, but even if he had she knew that, not even for her children, could she go back to that life of mindless servitude being Brad's wife had been. And she didn't intend marrying any man just to give her children a father either.

Andy pouted now. 'He said he likes to go swimming.'

'His name is Mr Thornton,' she rebuked. 'Or Sin, if you prefer,' she added ruefully, amazed at the easy way her children had taken to using the author's first name; she still had difficulty with it. 'And liking to go swimming and taking us with him are two different things.'

'But Sin said——'

'He was being polite, Andy,' she ruffled her son's hair affectionately, standing up. 'We could always pack a picnic and go down by the river, how would that be instead?'

She could see Andy was still having difficulty handling his disappointment, although he joined in readily enough once she and Kim began to plan the outing. Poor Andy, he was already suffering from a case of hero-worship. The next few weeks could be very difficult indeed.

'Robyn . . .?'

She turned sharply at the softly spoken query, having been unaware of Sin Thornton's ascent up the stairs as she laughed and joked with the children. 'Yes?' she frowned. Surely he wasn't the type of man to be offended by the ten minutes or so she had spent with Kim and Andy?

His hands rested on either side of the doorway as he filled the length and breadth of it. 'There's a telephone call for you,' he informed her softly.

Robyn instantly felt contrite for her suspicion. Of course Sin Thornton wasn't petty enough to be insulted by being left downstairs on his own for a few minutes; their laughter must have drowned out the sound of the telephone ringing.

'I'll take over here if you would like to go down and take the call,' Sin came further into the room, moving aside to let her exit.

'The twins will be fine on their own now,' she assured him.

'Nevertheless, I'll leave you to take the call in private.'

Something about the way he said the word 'private' made her view him sharply, colour entering her cheeks as the identity of her caller slowly seeped into her brain. Brad! It had to be Brad. The first time he had telephoned in weeks and it had to be when Sin Thornton was here. She could also understand Sin's reluctance to reveal her caller in front of the children; the lateness of the hour made it obvious Brad hadn't called to talk to Kim and Andy, knowing they would be in bed by now.

'I won't be long,' she assured him, knowing from experience that Brad's calls were never of long duration.

Sin merely nodded, already taking up the position she had vacated on Kim's bed, Robyn hearing her children's giggles of enjoyment at this change in routine as she hurried down the stairs. What could Brad be calling about at this late hour? He never telephoned to speak to her personally, although they usually managed a few polite words to each other before he spoke to the twins.

'Yes?' she spoke warily into the receiver as she stood in the hallway to take the call.

'Who's the man, Robyn?' Brad's mocking voice taunted without preamble.

Her mouth tightened, and she flushed resentfully. 'I don't think that's any of your business,' she snapped, finding it difficult to be polite to him even after all this time—and especially when he tried to pry into her personal life, something he had made it clear four years ago he had no interest in.

'Of course it's my business,' he rasped, the charm gone from his voice. 'I like to know what sort of men you're introducing to my children.'

Her breath caught in her throat. 'Meaning?' she bit out between clenched teeth, knowing her knuckles showed white as she clutched the receiver.

'Meaning they haven't mentioned to me yet having any "uncles",' he sneered. 'But I've been expecting it for some time.'

'Really?'

'Oh yes,' Brad scorned. 'You weren't always the cold little fish you are now.'

She blushed at the truth of that. She may have been inexperienced when they were first married but Brad had proved to be a good teacher when it came to the physical, tutoring her during the first months of their marriage in all the pleasures there could be between a man and a woman. The advent of her pregnancy had ended all that, though, Brad feeling only revulsion for the physical act with a woman fast growing big with his child. Once the twins had been born she was the one to feel the reluctance, feeling too tired to respond to him as she cared for the twins single-handed. She had known that during that time Brad turned to other women for his pleasure.

'I can't say I've felt desperate for a man the last four years,' she was stung into replying. 'And the man who answered the telephone just now is only a friend.'

'Who is he?'

'Brad, I can't believe you made this call just to ask me about my casual acquaintances,' she sighed her impatience, not willing to talk about Sin Thornton and involve him in something that was none of his business.

'It's how "casual" he is that bothers me,' her ex-husband drawled insultingly.

Robyn drew in an angry breath. 'He's a guest of your uncle's,' she snapped. 'Using the cottage next door.'

'Oh,' he dismissed any guest of his uncle's as not being in the least interesting. 'How is the old man?'

'Very well.'

'And Caroline?'

Robyn frowned. 'She's well too,' she answered in a preoccupied voice, wondering at the reason for this delay in the real reason Brad had telephoned; it certainly wasn't to discuss his uncle or Caroline! He usually came straight to the point, barely wasted time on pleasantries. In fact, this whole telephone call was out of character. 'The twins are in bed——'

'I know that,' he bit out abruptly. 'I

deliberately called when I knew they would be asleep——'

'They would have liked to talk to you——'

'—because I didn't want them to be around if you should prove to be difficult,' Brad finished as if he hadn't been interrupted.

Robyn stiffened warily. 'Difficult about what?' she asked slowly.

'You've had the kids to yourself completely for the last four years, and God knows I didn't interfere in the way you were bringing them up even when we were together——'

'Because you weren't interested!' she snapped.

'Maybe not,' he admitted grudgingly. 'But I'm not unique in that, a lot of men can't bring themselves to be interested in small babies the way women are. But Kim and Andy are older now, and——'

'You noticed,' she taunted nastily.

'Don't be bitter, Robyn,' he rasped.

'I'm not,' she sighed, some of her anger leaving her as she realised how badly she was behaving. 'I'm just wondering what it is you don't want me to be difficult about.' In fact, she was more than worried about it; she didn't like the sound of it at all.

Brad was silent for several lengthy seconds. 'I want the children for a weekend,' he finally told her.

His blunt statement rendered Robyn speechless. Whatever she had been expecting Brad to say it wasn't this! He had open access to the twins, she would never try and deny any of them the closeness a father should have with his children, but Brad had never even hinted before that he would like the children to go and stay with him in London, always visiting them here in the past while he stayed with the Colonel and Caroline.

She swallowed hard. 'What weekend?' to her chagrin her voice cracked a little, revealing how disconcerted she was by the request.

'Whenever it will suit you, of course,' Brad's relief at her relatively calm reaction could clearly be heard. 'And the twins,' he added pointedly.

That last comment had been deliberately designed to remind her that her own feelings of horror and dismay at the thought of her two children going away for the weekend had to be outweighed by the fact that Kim and Andy would be thrilled at the thought of going to stay with their father. London, and Brad's life there, held all sorts of wonders for the two five-year-olds. But Robyn couldn't help wondering, perhaps unfairly, at Brad's motives for issuing the invitation.

'Why, Brad?' the question came out bluntly.

'Why not?' he was instantly defensive. 'I am their father!'

Only through sheer effort of will could she hold back the sharp retort she felt tempted to make at the indignant declaration. It was true what she had told Sinclair Thornton earlier, she wasn't in the least bitter about the break-up of her marriage, but when she spoke to Brad she had difficulty hiding the bitterness she felt on the twins' behalf for his neglect of them all these years. And her suspicions about his reasons for this proposed visit had only intensified after his reaction to her question.

'So you are,' she acknowledged stiltedly. 'How long would this weekend be?'

'The usual Saturday to Sunday,' he taunted. 'I'll drive down on the Friday evening and we'll leave early Saturday.'

She drew in a ragged breath, the thought of being without the children even for that short length of time leaving her devastated. They had been a threesome for so long now, her responsibility to them total from the moment they were born, that she knew her life would be empty without them, even for two days. But she had to be fair to Brad and them, and if he really did feel more interested in them now that they were older who was she to deny them this further closeness? After all, what could possibly go wrong in two days? She determinedly pushed aside all the things that clamoured to be heard.

'This weekend is out,' she told him after careful thought. 'We've already made plans.' And tentative as they might be she needed the excuse to give herself the extra time to adjust to this change in all their lives. 'But if next weekend is all right with you I'm sure the twins would love to come.'

'Even if you won't like letting them,' Brad guessed dryly.

She sighed. 'I'll admit I find this sudden interest in the children a little—surprising.'

'I'll bet you do!'

She couldn't altogether blame Brad for his resentment, knew there had been too much between them in the past for them to talk on a personal level with any degree of politeness. It would always be that way between them, although she tried not to let Kim and Andy see it. 'Perhaps you would like to come to dinner Friday evening?' she suggested softly. 'The twins haven't seen you for some time, and it would help break the ice.'

'I'll accept the invitation, Robyn,' he told her harshly. 'Although I don't accept the fact that I need the ice broken with my own kids.'

He was really annoyed now, and if she didn't put an end to this call soon she knew from experience that they would rapidly resort to verbal abuse on such a level as to make the idea of sitting down to dinner together next Friday like an ordinary couple virtually impossible. It was always that way if they spoke for too long, and for the twins' sake she usually managed to avoid such scenes; tonight had to be no exception.

'Nevertheless, dinner together would be nice,' she insisted. 'The children would like it.'

'Okay,' he agreed in an offhand manner. 'But don't pin me down to a time, I'll be there when I can.'

She was used to the way Brad could never be on time for anything, and she would prepare a meal accordingly. 'We'll expect you when we see you,' she agreed.

'I'll leave it to you to tell Kim and Andy about next weekend.'

He would! 'I'll tell them,' she echoed.

'Until next Friday, then,' he said tersely at her lack of enthusiasm. 'I have to go now.'

'Of course,' she acknowledged abruptly, making her own curt goodbyes.

The twins were going to be overjoyed at the prospect of two whole days with their father in London, in fact she doubted she would be able to calm them down once they knew of the visit. But she was being selfish to think this way, any move Brad made to be a real father to Kim and Andy

had to be a welcome one. If only she knew the
reason for this sudden about-face on his part she
would feel happier about the situation. And if
only she could stop thinking in that negative way!
Brad may genuinely want to get to know his
children better. Then why did she have this
oppressive feeling in the pit of her stomach, the
feeling that something was wrong about all this?
Why did she question Brad's unusual behaviour
instead of just being thankful for Kim and
Andy's sake? It was——

'Problems?'

She turned sharply at the sound of that husky
query, only to find Sin Thornton leaning casually
against the bottom of the banister, one foot
resting on the bottom step as he watched her with
narrowed blue eyes. She had forgotten all about
her guest as she spoke to Brad!

CHAPTER THREE

SIN moved forward as she didn't answer, his expression turning to one of concern. 'Is everything all right, Robyn?' he probed again.

She straightened as she realised she was still chewing worriedly on her bottom lip, forcing a smile to curve her mouth. 'Everything is fine,' she answered lightly. 'That was Brad,' she told him as she led the way back into the lounge, knowing he was astute enough to have worked that out for himself.

'What did he want?'

Robyn's head came round sharply at the harshly spoken question. 'I don't think——'

'Sorry.' At once the charming smile was back on the roguishly handsome face. 'My curiosity getting the better of me again,' Sin added lightly.

Robyn wasn't at all convinced by this glib response to her indignation—although she couldn't think of any other reason for his interest in Brad and her conversation with him. She shook off her feelings of suspicion—she was feeling oversensitive after talking with Brad. She probably looked worried, and Sin was only showing a polite concern for her preoccupation.

'Hey, perhaps I'd better go——'

'No,' she cut in abruptly, realising what a bad hostess she was being. 'I don't have any brandy I can offer you, but I think there's still some wine left in the bottle we had with our meal . . .?' She looked at him enquiringly.

'Another cup of coffee would do me just as well,' Sin smiled acceptance of the offer.

Robyn nodded, frowning as she went into the kitchen. She had no idea how long Sin had been standing on the stairs behind her, or how much of her side of the conversation at least he had overheard. As she moved habitually about the kitchen preparing the coffee she tried to recall what she had said to Brad—and failed miserably. She had been so wrapped up in her own thoughts she hadn't been aware of what she was saying.

Not that it really mattered, somehow during the evening Sinclair Thornton had learnt nearly all there was about her to be learnt, including the break-up of her marriage and the identity of her ex-husband. Come to think of it, she had told him altogether too much!

'The twins are asleep, by the way,' Sin reported with a smile as they sat across the lounge from each other.

'How did you manage that?' she smiled took, having been sure her children would be too excited by their new acquaintance to fall asleep for hours yet.

Sin gave a grin of enjoyment. 'I think it was the story I told them.'

Her eyes widened; her offspring didn't usually fall asleep when being told a story, this one must have been particularly boring. 'What was it?'

He shrugged. 'The story is unimportant, it was the voice that did it.'

Robyn was still puzzled, unable to believe that liltingly charming voice could talk anyone to sleep.

'My brother has a couple of children too,' Sin explained. 'Talking them to sleep is a technique I

learnt I had when they were babies. I was quite
hurt by it for a time—until Kay, my sister-in-
law, told me what a Godsend it was. She has been
known to call me over in the middle of the night
when one of them is being particularly fretful,' he
grimaced ruefully.

'I'll bear that in mind,' she said dryly, sipping
her coffee in quiet contemplation.

'Feeling better now?'

She looked up with a frown. 'Hm?'

The blue eyes probed the slight flush to her
cheeks, the guarded look in her eyes. 'You were
upset when you came off the telephone,' he stated
bluntly.

'You're imagining things,' she dismissed
lightly. 'I was just surprised by the call, that's
all.'

'Is it?'

'Really, Sin, I don't think——'

'Neither do I.' He stood up abruptly. 'I'm
interfering in something that is obviously none of
my business.' He shook his head. 'It's just that
you seem so damned young to cope with all this
on your own. I thought you were no more than
sixteen when I met you this morning, and yet
tonight I find that you're a grown woman with
two young children of your own to care for. How
long is it since someone cared for *you*?'

Robyn was puzzled by his behaviour; he
seemed to be almost angry on her behalf. Which
was ridiculous, she hardly knew the man. 'I
don't think anyone ever did,' she replied slowly.
'My parents had the sort of marriage that was
complete without a child, and so I was put in
the charge of a series of nannies. When I
married Brad against their advice they disowned

me, said I was wasting the expensive education they had given me.' She sighed. 'They were right, I suppose. But having the twins has made up for a lot of things I missed out on as a child. I have no regrets about my life so far,' she assured him.

'Not even Brad Warner?'

'No, because without Brad there wouldn't be the twins,' she shrugged.

'That's true,' Sin acknowledged dryly. 'Well I'd better go—I think I've pushed my nose in where it's not wanted enough for one night. My mother tells me I was exactly the same as a child,' he derided. 'Although she assures me it isn't so endearing in an adult.'

His easy charm made it difficult for her to be offended by anything he said, although she did agree it was time he left. Sinclair Thornton was too easy to talk to, listened too well. Before she knew what was happening she would find herself as a character in one of his damned books; her life certainly hadn't been plain sailing so far. Remembering his reason for being here reminded her that he had only arrived here this morning.

'I'm sure you must be tired,' she stood up. 'I should have thought . . .'

'I'm thirty-seven, Robyn,' he mocked, the mischief back in his eyes. 'Not seventy-seven. A little bit of driving won't kill me.'

'I didn't mean——'

'I know you didn't,' he chuckled. 'Walk me to the door, hm?'

She felt much more at ease with this easygoing Sin, preferred not to have the probing questions that she seemed compelled to answer being thrown at her. 'You'll have to come over again before you leave,' she said politely once they reached the door.

'I hope so,' his eyes gleamed down at her in the bright moonlight. 'I know someone who is going to be very disappointed if I don't.'

'The twins,' she nodded.

'No—me!' He grinned down at her. 'I've enjoyed myself tonight. The three of you will have to come to me once I've settled in a little better. I'm a fantastic cook.'

'And modest with it!'

His amusement deepened. 'No one has ever accused me of being that.'

'I'm sure!'

The atmosphere suddenly became very still between them, all the laughter leaving Robyn's face as blue eyes held her captive. Her breath caught in her throat as she tried to break away from the intensity of that gaze, knowing she had lost the battle as lean hands moved out and slowly pulled her up and into a firmly muscled chest. Firm lips moved across hers, parting them as Sin took full advantage of her vulnerability, trapped as she was in his arms, her feet inches off the ground.

She felt so helpless, had never even guessed at the whipcord strength in the indolent body, muscular arms holding her in their vice-like grip. And most disturbing of all was her reaction to the pressure of warm lips moving erotically against her own, her senses quickening, the arms that had gone up about his neck as she felt her feet leave the ground now entwined against his nape, her fingers in the thickness of his golden hair. She was actually enjoying this physical contact with this wildly attractive man!

Her face was flushed, her eyes over-bright as
Sin raised his head to look down at her.

He smiled his satisfaction at her appearance. 'I
always like to thank my hostess in the appropriate
manner.'

The dreamy expression instantly left her face,
as she pushed against his chest to be released, her
mouth tightening as she was made aware of his
arousal on her slow journey down to the ground.
'Consider her thanked,' she snapped. 'I'm sure
Caroline will be suitably impressed.'

Sin frowned, reluctant to release her completely, his hands still firmly on her waist.
'Caroline . . .?'

She nodded. 'When you go up to the Hall for
dinner. You are going, aren't you?' she added
waspishly, angry with herself for feeling even a
moment of weakness towards this man.

'Tomorrow. But——'

'Have a good time.' She ran her hands down
her thighs once she was free of him, ashamed of
their slight dampness. 'The Colonel has a very
good cook, and I'm sure the company will be
very agreeable.' She was so angry—at herself and
him—that her voice still shook with it.

'I'm sure I will.' His frown had turned to a
dark scowl. 'Robyn——'

'I must go in,' she interrupted firmly. 'The
light from the hallway is attracting the moths and
things.' The latter was true, but they both knew
that wasn't her real reason for going back into the
cottage. 'Thank you for the tulips. Caroline's
favourite flowers are carnations, by the way,' she
added brittly. 'Pink ones.'

'Caroline is a child——'

'You thought I was one too until a few hours

ago,' she reminded him forcefully. 'And yet that didn't stop you flirting with me this morning.'

Sin's mouth tightened as a dull red colour slowly ebbed into his cheeks. 'That was only a little harmless fun——'

'Not to a sixteen-year-old it wouldn't have been!'

'Robyn, you're seeing this out of proportion——'

'I'm not "seeing" it at all, that's the problem,' she glared at him. 'I left behind the casual encounters you're obviously accustomed to when I moved here from London!'

'For God's sake,' he snapped his exasperation. 'I kissed you goodnight, not raped you!'

'I've been a divorcee for two years,' she scorned derisively. 'And you know how a woman alone is apt to see more into these things than she should!'

'I don't believe that any more than you do,' he sighed. 'Although I'm sorry such a fleeting kiss has caused so much hassle.'

'For you or for me?'

'Both!'

'Try your charm on Caroline, Mr Thornton,' she scoffed. 'She makes no secret of her attraction to older, more sophisticated men.'

'Thanks!'

'I believe in honesty,' Robyn bit out.

'So do I—in moderation,' he added with rueful humour, the gleam back in his startling blue eyes. 'I'm not going to push my luck any further tonight where you're concerned, I'm quitting while I'm ahead.'

Robyn was surprised that he thought he was, she had the distinct impression she had very

firmly put him in his place. He didn't seem to
agree with her. And as she lay in bed later that
night it was that kiss that bothered her,
tormented her until she couldn't sleep, not worry
over Brad's unexpected deepening of interest in
their children.

She was running late. It had been inevitable after
she had switched off the ringing of the alarm at
six-thirty, turning over with a groan to fall back
into a deep sleep until Kim and Andy came
bouncing into her room shortly after seven. After
that it had been one mad dash to try and catch up
with herself, seeing to the twins' needs, putting
on the washing, feeding the cat—and all before
she could even start to think of dressing herself
and getting ready to go to work. Thank God it
was Friday, at least tomorrow she could have a
legitimate lay-in until seven-thirty, maybe eight
o'clock if she were lucky!

As a consequence she wasn't pleased when the
knock sounded firmly on the cottage door at a
quarter to nine, knowing she needed all the time
before nine o'clock to get herself ready. Surely
the milkman didn't want paying today; he usually
waited until Saturday morning, when he could be
sure of finding her at home.

It wasn't the milkman who stood on the
doorstep, and she pulled her robe more securely
about her, conscious of the worn brown velour
garment as Sin Thorton's eyes widened at her
appearance, making no effort to hide his interest
in the creamy skin exposed by the vee-neckline of
the cotton nightgown she wore beneath the robe.

'I thought you were the milkman,' she felt
flustered into saying something.

'Really?'

The ludicrousness of the situation struck her at the same moment Sin drawled the suggestive query, and suddenly she was giggling like the schoolgirl she had denied being.

'Come in,' she invited once she was a little more controlled. 'Before the neighbours get the wrong impression,' she added teasingly, her rancour of last night forgotten for the moment in their shared humour.

'This one already has,' Sin grinned as he preceded her into the kitchen.

'Tough!' she drawled. 'Now what can I do for you? As you can see, I'm not dressed yet,' and felt decidedly *un*dressed next to the casual but obviously expensively cut navy blue shirt and grey trousers he wore. 'And I have to be at work in——' she glanced at the big kitchen clock on the wall, '—twenty minutes,' she told him with a grimace.

'You're cutting it a bit fine, aren't you?' He raised blond brows, seeming to dominate her small kitchen.

'Tell me something I don't know,' she glared at him.

'Your robe is undone.'

She gasped, looking down to find her robe securely in place, the belt neatly tied at her slender waist. She looked up at Sin with accusing eyes, finding he really did live up to his name at that moment, his eyes gleaming with wicked satisfaction.

'Got your interest, though, didn't I,' he mocked unrepentantly.

'You've got that anyway—for two minutes. Then I throw you out,' she warned.

'Should be interesting.'

'You think I can't do it?' her voice was deceptively soft as she issued the challenge.

'Please,' Sin held up his hands defensively. 'I came here to make my peace, not have another argument.'

She raised auburn brows. 'Have we argued?'

'Not going to make this easy for me, are you?' he realised self-derisively.

'What?' Robyn feigned innocence.

He gave a rueful smile. 'I give up! I just wanted to say I'm sorry about last night, in retrospect I realise I came on a bit strong for our first evening together. You're right about the company I keep in London; I forgot where I was for a while—and that you had obviously opted out of that casually intimate way of life.'

Robyn flushed at the latter, until that moment having been preoccupied with the term 'first evening together', almost as if he expected there to be a lot more of them. Well she had news for him, once Caroline got her claws into him none of his evenings would be free!

'I haven't opted out of that way of life,' she told him stiffly. 'Because I never joined it. Brad was the first man I ever dated seriously——'

'And since then?'

She met his gaze unflinchingly. 'Since then is no one's business but my own.'

'And the man involved, I would presume,' Sin mocked.

'Yes,' she agreed flatly, not correcting his assumption that there *was* a man. He *had* come on too strong last night, and she didn't want a repeat of it now or at any other time. He had made his obligatory pass, she intended making sure there was no mistake about him needing to make another one.

'I'd better leave you to get ready for work,' he nodded, turning to go.

'Thanks for coming round.' She walked him to the door, relieved at his acceptance of the situation.

He shrugged. 'My pleasure. And, Robyn . . .?'

'Yes?' she looked up at him enquiringly.

Devilment glittered in the dark blue eyes. '*What* did you say were Caroline's favourite flowers?'

Her mouth curved into an amused smile. This man was impossible! 'Pink carnations,' she laughed. 'As you well know,' she added sternly.

'As I well know,' Sin grinned. 'I'll be seeing you,' came his parting shot before he strode across the grass to the cottage next door.

Not too soon, she hoped. She had enough on her mind at the moment without having to worry about crossing verbal swords with the irrepressible Sinclair Thornton every two minutes.

But it seemed it was already impossible for him not to have altered the even tenor of her life, as she found out later that morning when Caroline came into her office.

'How did yesterday evening go?' Caroline came straight to the point, her tone condescending, obviously expecting to hear that it had been a disaster from start to finish.

Robyn looked up fatalistically, having been expecting Caroline for the last hour, although she could have wished the other woman had chosen some other time to come and harass her; she needed her attention on the job in hand when she was doing the wages for the estate workers. 'Very well, thank you,' she answered noncommittally.

Caroline's mouth tightened. 'I'm sure Sin was bored out of his mind,' she scorned.

She stiffened, although the other woman's attitude really came as no surprise to her; Caroline must have been furious when Sin had refused her dinner invitation yesterday in favour of her own! 'He didn't seem to be,' she shrugged.

Caroline gave her a pitying glance. 'I'm sure he was too polite to show it.'

'You'll have to ask him, won't you,' Robyn sighed, having no patience for this sort of confrontation today. 'When you see him tonight,' she added pointedly.

'I don't envisage discussing you at all tonight, or those brats of yours,' the other woman dismissed haughtily. 'It's enough that you were impolite enough to put one of my father's guests in such an awkward position in the first place.'

Robyn flushed at the barb. 'I've already explained about that——'

'I know,' Caroline snapped. 'But Daddy would appreciate it if you didn't interfere in that way again.'

She felt sure it was really the younger woman who wanted no interference where Sinclair Thornton was concerned, that having actually met the man she now wanted him as her lover. Not that she could really blame Caroline for that, Sin was very attractive. But she had a feeling Sin would prefer to do his own choosing about the women in his life, that he was a man who liked to do the chasing, not the other way around.

'Think of it this way, Caroline,' she drawled. 'At least now you have a chance to get your hair done before tonight.'

The perfectly bowed mouth tightened perceptively. 'As it happens I do have an appointment this afternoon,' Caroline confirmed resentfully. 'Did the terrible twins behave themselves last night?' she added with relish.

'They aren't terrible,' she bit out hardly. 'And of course they behaved themselves.'

'Don't sound so indignant,' the younger woman derided. 'I wouldn't be surprised by anything those two did.'

'Then you *won't* be surprised to know that they were perfectly well behaved!'

Caroline smiled her satisfaction at having once again managed to get under Robyn's skin. 'Parental love speaking, darling,' she dismissed.

'I don't think so——'

'Of course you don't,' the younger woman laughed scornfully. 'You're the parent. Which reminds me, your husband——'

'Ex-husband,' she corrected tautly.

'Ex-husband,' Caroline repeated mockingly. 'He telephoned Daddy this morning and invited himself down next Friday for the night.'

'Yes.'

'You don't seem surprised?'

'I'm not,' Robyn confirmed.

'I don't know why he can't stay with you down at the cottage——'

'Because we only have the two bedrooms!'

'So?'

'So it would be a little crowded with the three of them in the twins' room,' she bit out between clenched teeth.

'Really, Robyn, how old fashioned you are. Don't you know that everyone is sleeping with their ex nowadays?' Caroline said in a bored voice.

'I'm not everyone,' she returned curtly.

'No, you aren't, are you,' she managed to make it sound like an insult. 'What is this anyway, Brad's usual quarterly visit?' she scoffed.

Robyn's fingers tightened about the pen she held clasped in her hand. 'You'll have to ask him that.'

'Oh, I intend to,' Caroline smiled without humour. 'There's nothing I enjoy more than an intimate conversation with my cousin.'

It was a well known fact that Brad and Caroline argued every occasion that they met, and no doubt Caroline would enjoy baiting Brad as to the reason for this visit. Robyn only hoped she was told the reason before the younger, bitchier woman, as she hated to feel at a disadvantage where Caroline was concerned.

'Was that all, Caroline?' she sighed. 'I have to finish off the wages.'

The younger woman's mouth tightened with irritation. 'I only came to tell you Daddy wants you in his study as soon as you have a moment.'

And to question her about the evening with Sin! Caroline had the subtlety of a battering ram. 'I'll go through in a moment,' she nodded. 'Nothing wrong, is there?' she frowned, wondering if it had anything to do with Brad's proposed visit.

'You'll have to ask Daddy that, won't you,' Caroline dismissed with relish, obviously enjoying Robyn's worried expression.

One of these days——! She seemed to be saying that a lot lately where Caroline was concerned, and she had a feeling that day wasn't going to be long coming. And when it did come she may just find herself out of a home and job.

Damn the woman, why didn't she move up to London permanently instead of just the occasional weekend! Life had certainly been a lot more peaceful before Caroline came home for good.

Peace. Was that really all she wanted from life? She had thought that she did—Of course she did! She was just a little unsettled at the moment, worried about Brad, angered by these constant verbal battles with Caroline. Envious of the younger woman's carefree life? No! But was she? She hadn't thought so, had no idea why the question had come into her mind, loved the twins more than life itself. But didn't she occasionally wish she didn't have the responsibility of providing a home and living for them all, didn't she resent the fact that Caroline had everything given to her on a silver platter, that life hadn't dealt her any of the knocks Robyn had had to deal with the last few years? Of course she felt that, she wouldn't be human if she didn't! But she felt sure she wouldn't like, or find Caroline's bitchiness any more tolerable, if she were still living her own pampered existence with her father and mother. The two would certainly have no more in common than they did now.

And right now she had to go and see the Colonel, knowing that 'when she had a moment' meant as soon as she could in the Colonel's language. She knocked softly on the adjoining door, entering after a polite lapse. Sin Thornton stood alone in the room, turning from his contemplation of the extensive gardens.

'Hi,' he greeted lightly.

'Hello,' her own greeting was much more guarded, looking around pointedly for the Colonel.

'He had to step out of his study for a moment,' Sin explained. 'A problem in the Gift Shop, I think.'

'Oh.' She felt awkward just standing there, but she had been disconcerted by Sin's presence here when she had expected to see the Colonel. 'Maybe I'd better come back later,' she suggested.

'No,' Sin's hand on her arm was firm. 'He shouldn't be very long.'

'But I'm sure he won't want me to intrude on your meeting——'

'On the contrary,' Sin drawled, his hand dropped away to be thrust into the hip pocket of his fitted trousers. 'We were talking about you, actually.'

'Me?' her eyes widened indignantly as she wondered what had been said.

'Don't look so outraged,' Sin mused. 'What we were actually discussing was the Colonel's secretary——'

'But that is me——'

'—and the fact that she could help me with my research,' he finished pointedly.

Robyn's frown deepened. 'Me?'

'You're beginning to sound repetitious,' he mocked.

She flushed at the taunt. 'I don't understand how I can help with your research. Your books are all blood and thunder, aren't they?' she said with distaste.

'I've never thought of them in that way,' he frowned, his humour fading.

'Then maybe you should!'

'Maybe,' he bit out, aware of her censure. 'But the research I have in mind is of a purely historical nature. Of course, I usually do it all myself——'

'Then why not this time?' She was rankled at the way he and the Colonel seemed to have made this decision for her; she already had enough to do as secretary and part-time guide.

He shrugged broad shoulders beneath the navy blue shirt. 'It's Henry's idea——'

Henry! Already he was calling the older man by his first name; she had known Brad's uncle for six years and she *still* called him the Colonel!

'—that while I'm talking to him in the afternoons you could do some of the research for me,' Sin seemed unaware of her wandering thoughts as he continued speaking. 'Of course, if you would rather not . . .'

They both knew she would rather not! 'It isn't a question of that,' she said stiffly. 'I have other work to do in the afternoons.'

'Ah yes,' Sin nodded. 'Taking around the interested public. Henry thought Caroline could do that for a couple of weeks.'

It would almost be worth it just to see the younger woman's face! But the thought of working with, and for, Sinclair Thornton certainly detracted from that pleasure. 'Has he told Caroline yet?' she mused.

'Not yet. He didn't want to do anything about that until he'd spoken to you.'

'You mean I have a choice in the matter?'

'Everyone has choices, Robyn,' he spoke quietly.

She had the feeling he wasn't talking about doing his research at that moment. And she couldn't for the life of her think what he *was* talking about! 'Caroline will not be pleased,' she stated with certainty.

Sin shrugged. 'From what Henry told me she doesn't have a lot else to do around here.'

Robyn spluttered with laughter. 'She doesn't want anything to do!'

'Doesn't she get bored?'

'I have no idea, we aren't exactly into those sort of confidences,' she derided, sure that Caroline was never bored, even though she never so much as read a book or did anything more strenuous than enjoying herself. 'Why don't you ask her to help you with your research?' an imp of devilment urged her to suggest.

Sin's mouth twisted as he guessed at her mockery. 'Henry assures me his daughter isn't into reading anything deeper than a woman's magazine.'

'Surely that depends who the author is?'

The blue eyes gleamed as he smiled. 'I wish I could believe your flattery was genuine,' he drawled.

Her brows rose. 'You don't think it is?'

'I know it isn't,' he chuckled. 'But——'

'Sorry about that,' the Colonel came into the room, a small portly man with a red-flushed face and silver-white hair, the neatly trimmed moustache adding to his image, the pale blue eyes bright with a shrewdness that had kept the estate intact for Caroline and any heirs she might have. 'Ah, Robyn,' he smiled at her. 'I hope you've kept our guest entertained?'

She glanced over at the laughing blue eyes, thinking crossly that Sinclair Thornton never seemed to be anything else; the whole of life seemed to be one big game to him. 'I've tried to,' she murmured softly.

'And you've succeeded,' he mocked her as he seemed to read her thoughts.

The Colonel looked from one to the other of them, as if sensing there was more to the conversation than at first appeared. He shrugged his wide shoulders in dismissal of the idea at their bland expressions. 'What do you think of the idea of helping Sin, Robyn?' he enquired briskly.

'I'm not really sure I would be much help——'

'You're being modest, Robyn,' Sin put in smoothly. 'Henry tells me you were a history student before your marriage.'

She looked accusingly at the older man, not appreciating being discussed in this way in her absence. 'Three months' study hardly qualifies me as a history student,' she snapped her displeasure.

'It means you're interested in it,' Sin insisted.

'But not in glorifying the less pleasant parts of it,' she met the deep blue eyes in challenge.

'You won't be writing the story, Robyn, I will,' Sin reminded her softly, the atmosphere suddenly very tense in the small room. 'All I'll require from you is clearly written dates and facts from the Colonel's diaries.'

She had seen those huge volumes in the extensive library, had shuddered to think of all the needless pain and suffering chronicled between their covers. To have to actually read them filled her with horror. The Colonel could be a kind and understanding man, was obviously lovingly indulgent with his only child, but when it came to matters of the world war he had served in he was truly of the old school, had never forgotten a battle or a campaign in all the following years.

'You've read them?' she asked Sin quietly.

'Several months ago,' he nodded, his eyes

narrowed on her pale face. 'Henry very kindly sent them to me in London.'

'Robyn is a little squeamish when it comes to the war,' the Colonel told him with amusement.

'Perhaps it's understandable—in the circumstances,' Sin was still watching her closely.

'Circumstances?' the Colonel frowned. 'Oh you mean Brad's escapades all over the world,' he dismissed. 'Hardly the same thing, old boy. We were out there making history, Brad simply reports it.'

'Would you rather not do this, Robyn?' Sin ignored the older man's callous dismissal of her emotions. 'I'm sure I can find the time to do it myself if you——'

'Nonsense,' the Colonel once again dismissed, his voice authoritative. 'Can't bury your head in the sand like an ostrich all your life,' he told them briskly. 'It's time you grew out of this, Robyn,' he ordered. 'Maybe if you did that husband of yours would come home where he belongs.'

'Ex-husband, Colonel,' she reminded awkwardly, giving Sin an uncomfortable look from beneath lowered lashes. 'Brad and I are divorced.'

'Don't believe in them myself,' he shook his head, as if that made them null and void. 'A marriage is for life, not to be discarded when it doesn't suit you.'

She couldn't agree more, unfortunately Brad didn't feel the same way, and no one could even try to keep a marriage alive when only one of the partners was participating.

'I'm sure you're pleased about his visit next weekend, whatever you say,' the Colonel beamed.

Robyn deliberately didn't look at Sin Thornton

this time, although she sensed his quickening interest. He had the answer to last night's questions after all, compliments of the Colonel! Sometimes she felt as if she were living her life in a goldfish bowl. 'The twins will be pleased to see him,' she evaded giving her own views on the subject, sensitive to this man's relationship to the man who had once been her husband.

'The twins, bah,' her uncle-by-marriage scoffed forcefully. 'There's no shame in admitting you'll be glad to see him too,' he chided.

After the way Brad had let her down repeatedly in their marriage she didn't particularly care if she never saw him again, but she could hardly be so blunt to his uncle. 'I'm sure we will all have a pleasant time,' she was still evasive, conscious of their avid audience. 'When do you want me to start work for you, Mr Thornton?' she enquired coolly, her gaze steady on his as she turned to look at him.

'Monday—if that suits you, Henry?' he turned to the other man.

'Fine, fine,' the Colonel beamed, his pride obvious in being chosen as the subject for one of the famous author's books.

Robyn could understand his feelings even if she didn't share them, more and more convinced that she herself could appear as a particularly colourful character in one of Sin's books.

She gave a cool inclination of her head. 'Until Monday, then, Mr Thornton.'

As she left the room, moving with quiet dignity, her head held high, she was very conscious of questioning blue eyes following her every movement.

CHAPTER FOUR

'WHY the hell didn't you tell me?'

Robyn watched in open-mouthed amazement as Sin pushed past her into the cottage after she had answered his imperious knock, following him dazedly as he went through to the lounge. He looked furious as he turned in front of the unlit fireplace to face her, although the sight of how handsome he looked in the black evening suit and snowy white shirt momentarily robbed her of speech. Even Caroline, for all her affected sophistication, would have had to have been impressed by the wide shoulders shown to advantage beneath the expensive material, his tapered waist and thighs, his legs long and lean.

But Caroline's feelings about this man weren't important to Robyn right now, the reason he had arrived on her doorstep at almost eleven o'clock at night breathing fire was! 'Why the hell didn't I tell you what?' she demanded. 'And will you kindly keep your voice down,' she hissed. 'I have two children asleep upstairs. At least, they were,' she added pointedly, his arrival several seconds ago in the silver-grey Porsche in the adjoining driveway not exactly done quietly, neither had his exit from the car been, as he slammed the door behind him.

'Sorry,' he bit out impatiently, although he lowered his voice considerably, his jacket pushed back as he thrust his hands into his trouser pockets. 'And why didn't you tell me about your ex-husband?'

'Brad?' she realised dazedly. Whatever explanation she had been expecting for his strange behaviour it certainly hadn't been this! If he had wanted to discuss Brad's proposed visit for next weekend that the Colonel had revealed why hadn't he come over earlier, instead of barging in here this late at night? The answer to that was all too obvious; the twins had still been up when Sin left in the Porsche for dinner at the main house, allowed to stay up later on a Friday evening. But what made Sin think it was any of his business in the first place she had no idea! 'I don't know what right you think you have to question me on such a personal subject,' she bit out icily. 'My ex-husband's visits to our children are none of your business. And if you think that kiss of last night makes it your business then you couldn't be more wrong! I——'

'What are you talking about?' he interrupted tersely. 'Who mentioned the damned visit?'

'You did——'

'No,' he shook his head.

She frowned her puzzlement. 'But just now——'

'I wanted to know why you didn't think to mention the fact that your ex-husband is the Colonel's nephew!'

'Oh.' The colour slowly ebbed into her cheeks as she realised how stupidly vain she had been. Of course Sinclair Thornton hadn't seen more into the casual kiss they had shared than there really was, it certainly hadn't been enough for him to assume he had any rights in her life.

Sin's mouth quirked as he correctly assessed her embarrassment. 'Flattering yourself, weren't you?' he mocked, the laughter back in his eyes.

'I was—mistaken,' she admitted awkwardly, feeling ridiculous for her assumption. 'And I didn't mention Brad's relationship to the Colonel because it didn't seem relevant.'

'It's very relevant when I've been shooting my mouth off about what a swine your husband was to have left you alone to cope as he has!'

Now it was Robyn's turn to enjoy his discomfort, smiling broadly. 'Did you do that?'

'Yes,' he scowled. 'And don't look so amused, I could have lost the Colonel's co-operation because of it!'

Robyn instantly sobered. 'I don't think so,' she shook her head. 'He's enjoying revelling in the past.'

'You can't blame him and every man like him for Brad's chasing of the next big story,' Sin said gently.

She turned away. 'I don't, I'm not that neurotic, no matter what impression the Colonel may have given you. It just seems to me that enough has already been written and said on the subject of war.'

'Considering you have no idea of the theme my book is going to take don't you think that's rather a sweeping statement to have made?' he rebuked softly.

Once again he had succeeded in making her feel small and petty. 'Probably,' she conceded. 'I hope my omission about Brad didn't put you in too awkward a position.'

'Do you?'

'Yes,' she snapped at his lack of faith in her.

'I managed to smooth it over,' he shrugged.

She was sure he had, Sin had enough charm to get himself out of any situation. 'I didn't think you would be back for hours yet,' she changed the subject, grimacing at his mocking expression. 'If I thought about it at all,' she added dismissively, realising too late that she had revealed her interest in his movements.

Sin crossed his arms across the broadness of his chest. 'Admit it, you thought about it.'

'Now who's flattering whose self?' she drawled.

His smile deepened, and Robyn was relieved to see he was one of those people who didn't hold grudges. 'Do you have any coffee made?' he asked hopefully.

'Didn't Caroline provide you with any?' she returned bitchily.

'Jealous?'

'Don't be ridiculous,' she denied agitatedly, wondering why this man persisted in flirting with her when everything she said and did rejected him.

'Wishful thinking,' he grimaced ruefully. 'You didn't answer my question about coffee,' he reminded.

'Instant?' she returned reluctantly.

'Fine.' He followed her as she set about preparing it. 'I live on this stuff when I'm actually working,' he admitted.

Robyn turned to look at him. 'Aren't you writing now?'

He shook his head. 'Not for months yet. I write one book a year, and I make sure it's thoroughly researched first.'

The reminder that this time she was to help him with that made her mouth tighten. 'Have you broken the news to Caroline yet that she's to become a tour guide in the afternoons?' she raised her brows questioningly.

'I can't see what you were worried about,' he shrugged. 'She took it very well.'

She would, in front of this man, but no doubt Robyn would hear more on the subject after the weekend.

'For a girl who was silently gnashing her teeth,' Sin added with amusement.

Robyn looked at him in surprise, finding Sin grinning back broadly, unable to repress her own humour as she burst out laughing. Their shared laughter eased what little tension there was left between them, and as if by mutual consent they carried their drinks into the lounge and sat down next to each other on the sofa.

'Miss Masters isn't a girl who likes to be told what to do,' Sin mused, still smiling.

'She isn't usually so revealing of her feelings.'

'I think we took her unawares.'

'As you did me!' she recalled irritably, her humour fading fast.

'You were even more obvious than Caroline was.'

'I meant to be!'

'I know it,' he sipped at his coffee. 'What time shall I call for you tomorrow?'

'I don't work Saturdays.'

'I don't mean to work. My, how you misunderstand me. I—Do you mind if I take off my jacket and tie?' he ran a finger beneath his buttoned collar as if to demonstrate its uncomfortableness. 'It's a warm night.'

She only just held back from pointing out the fact that it was almost morning, not night! It might be late, but she couldn't be that impolite. 'Go ahead,' she invited, and then wished she hadn't as he proceeded to peel the jacket from his body, revealing just how fitted to his muscular physique the white silk shirt was, the bow-tie at his throat quickly following the jacket over the arm of a neighbouring chair before he released the top three buttons of his shirt. The skin on his chest was deeply tanned, the wiry hair there made to look even more golden against its darkness.

'That's better.' His arm moved along the back of the sofa behind her as he turned to face her. 'Now where were we?' he looked thoughtful. 'Ah yes,' his brow cleared. 'Tomorrow. Have you forgotten we're all going swimming together?'

She had tried to forget the casually mentioned invitation, although Kim and Andy had made that impossible, reminding her of it even as she had put them to bed this evening. 'Don't feel you have to be obliged to take us,' she assured him. 'The twins did put you in a corner.'

'One I could quite easily have got out of if I had wanted to. Don't be deceived by the easygoing man you see before you,' he grinned. 'I've never been made to do, either by force or coercion, anything I didn't want to do.'

She could believe that, was already aware that the charm and humour hid a will of steel, that this man would always find a way of achieving exactly what he wanted to do.

'Are you going to try and stop me doing something I desperately want to do now?'

Her head rose sharply at the husky query, suddenly finding herself drowning in the sensuality of deep blue eyes that were only inches from her own. She moistened her lips nervously. 'That really depends on what you want to do,' her own voice came out huskily too.

'Kiss you.'

She had known that before she asked the question, had merely hoped to delay the moment. '*Could* I stop you?' she said inevitably.

'No,' he chuckled, his face suddenly going out of focus as he moved close enough for his mouth to totally possess and claim hers.

His kisses had exactly the same effect as they had the previous evening—they were devastating! And this time he had no intention of being satisfied with one kiss, parting her lips to deeply plunder the warm recesses of her mouth, his arms like steel about her until he sensed her lack of resistance, tasting her mouth now, sipping deeply from the nectar even as one of his hands moved to cup her full breast.

She felt her body melt at the intimacy of his touch, could feel his warmth through the thinness of her cotton shirt and lacy bra, groaned into his mouth as her nipple tautened against his palm, a temptation to his questing fingertips.

'I've wanted this since the moment I first saw you,' he muttered against her throat, releasing the top two buttons of her shirt to smooth the material away from her heated flesh. 'Robyn? Do you want it too?'

Did she want what? This wildfire excitement, the intimacy of his kisses, his sensual caresses? Yes, she wanted those things so badly, but she didn't want the emotions that went with them. And she certainly didn't want any more than caresses from him; she had only met the man *yesterday*!

Even as she realised that she was pushing him away, unaware of her flushed beauty as she looked up at him with shadowed brown eyes. She

was behaving like a wanton with a complete
stranger, and——

'Hey,' he chided softly as the tension left his
body. 'Nothing happened,' he reassured her as
she remained pale.

No, nothing had really happened—except in
her mind! God, how she had *wanted* in her mind,
had never known such instantaneous desire, her
body still trembling with it! 'No,' she acknowledged shakily. 'How about earlier?' she looked at
him with challenging eyes.

His brows rose as he took his time about
answering. 'Earlier?' he prompted.

'Were you any more successful with Caroline?'
she bit out insultingly.

Only the hardening of glittering blue eyes
betrayed just how angry he was, otherwise he
remained relaxed. 'Caroline is a very friendly
girl,' he drawled.

'So I've heard.' Robyn moved completely away
from him, sitting stiffly on the edge of the sofa to
rebutton her shirt, flinching as long fingers gently
caressed the hair away from her throbbing temple.

'I really am too old for her, Robyn,' Sin told
her throatily. 'Am I too old for you too?'

She frowned. 'Don't be ridiculous.'

'Thirteen years,' he shrugged. 'Almost a whole
generation's difference.'

'Your age has nothing to do with—with—Your
age isn't important,' she amended irritably.

'But the fact that I'm rushing you is.' He stood
up in fluid movements. 'I didn't mean to come
here tonight and upset you again.' He pulled on
his jacket, pushing the bow-tie into his pocket.
'Put it down to the fact that I can't seem to keep
my hands off you!'

Her cheeks flushed fiery red at the admission. 'Do you try very hard?' she feebly tried to lighten the conversation as it became too serious for her to handle with any degree of decorum.

He drew in a ragged breath, his gaze steady on hers. 'Do I have to?'

'I'm not sure,' she admitted honestly.

'You still love him, is that it?'

'Brad?'

'Well so far he's the only "him" you've admitted to having in your life!'

She gave a deep sigh. 'He is, and has been, the only "him" in my life.' Until now, she added silently.

'Then you do still love him,' the statement was made flatly, Sin's expression just as unrevealing.

She had never felt that she needed to explain her marriage to anyone, wasn't sure she wanted to now, but it seemed to be important to this man to know. And somehow that made it important to her too. 'When I first married Brad I had stars in my eyes, was in love with the idea of love,' she began softly. 'And when the marriage began to fall apart after only a few months I blamed him, his job, the fact that it took him away from me all the time, into a world I couldn't and didn't want to be part of. I accused him of not needing me, of needing his job more—until I realised I had it all wrong, that it was *I* who didn't need him.' There was raw pain in her eyes as she admitted to Sin something she had been afraid to admit to herself the first few months after she and Brad parted. 'I told you about my parents, the fact that I wasn't really necessary to their marriage? Well all my life I was searching for someone who needed and loved *me*, and I thought that with Brad I had found that someone.' She shrugged. 'Maybe if I hadn't become pregnant with the twins our marriage would have continued indefinitely, me still in love with love, Brad having a woman available whenever he chose to come home. But the twins' birth was something Brad had never wanted, in fact he——' she repressed a shudder as she remembered Brad's suggestion that she destroy the twins growing inside her. 'Well, he was a man who had no interest in having children,' she amended, although she could see by the narrowing of dark blue eyes that Sin had guessed at her unfinished sentence. 'I couldn't blame him for that,' she shrugged. 'Not when I realised it was exactly what I *had* wanted, that now I had them to love and care for my life was complete.'

'And you no longer needed Brad?' Sin prompted.

'He was no longer in our lives to be needed,' she revealed painfully. 'At least, officially he was, unofficially I didn't see him for months at a time. We all lived here while he stayed in the apartment in London. Twice when I—when I telephoned him there a different woman answered, and when I told her I was Mrs Warner she assumed I was Brad's mother! Obviously he had omitted to mention that he was a married man, and I didn't enlighten them. Brad and I were two people who married for all the wrong reasons—thank God we had the sense not to stay together for them too!'

'So you aren't in love with him?'

'No,' she confirmed.

'But there's never been another man in your life since him?'

She flushed. 'No.'

'Because you still don't need a man in your life, is that it?' his eyes were narrowed once again.

'You know I responded to you——'

'That isn't what I'm saying, Robyn, and you know it.' He sat down beside her once again, smoothing back her tousled hair. 'Physically I'm sure I could make you accept me——'

'You——'

'Please, Robyn, let me finish,' he interrupted her outrage. 'I'm not a boy, I *know* I could make you want me. But I want more than that——'

'After only two days?' she scoffed any deeper feelings than desire.

'After two minutes,' he corrected softly.

She swallowed hard at the quiet determination in his voice. 'You were right the first time, Sin, I don't need a man in my life,' she said hardly.

'How about if one forces his way in?'

She shook her head. 'I don't think he—you, could do that.'

'All right, lovely lady,' he smoothed the frown from her brow, smiling gently. 'I won't push you any more for now, I think I've given you enough to think about for one night,' he added with a satisfied grin.

He knew damned well that he had! For the second night in succession she found it difficult to sleep, to put one maddeningly irritating man out of her mind. She still didn't know quite what Sin wanted from her, certainly a physical relationship, although he seemed to demand more than that, wanted her emotions to be involved as well as her body. And after years of suppressing both she couldn't give him either!

*　　*　　*

'This is not the way to the local pool,' she turned to Sin with a puzzled frown as he directed the car away from the town instead of towards it.

'No,' he confirmed he was well aware of the fact, relaxed and confident behind the wheel of the Porsche.

He had knocked on the adjoining cottage wall fifteen minutes ago, arriving on the doorstep a couple of minutes later, the sun glinting on the gold of his overlong hair, his fitted shirt that colour that was neither blue nor green, giving his eyes the same glow, the low-fitting denims faded and worn. Robyn hadn't needed to be told he had come to take them swimming, and with the twins hopping and jumping about in the background it had been impossible not to go along with the plan.

Although she hadn't wanted to. After last night she felt more justified in keeping her distance from Sin Thornton. He wanted a relationship with her she wasn't prepared to give, made demands on her emotions that would just leave her hurting once he had left Colton and forgotten that she and the twins existed.

But Kim and Andy's excitement when they realised the proposed swimming trip was definitely on had been too much for her to deny them this treat, and even now their pleasure couldn't be suppressed as they sat in the back of the car, the picnic basket Robyn had packed in preparation for their original plan to drive down to the river on the seat beside them, Sin assuring them they would find somewhere to sit and eat the food.

Robyn frowned even more as Sin manoeuvred the car into the constant stream of traffic on the motorway. 'I thought we were going swimming?'

'We are,' he nodded.

'Where?'

'To the coast.'

Her gasp of surprise was drowned out as Kim and Andy whooped their delight. The nearest thing resembling a coastal resort was fifty miles away, and it was last summer since Robyn had been able to take them there. The length of the journey there and back meant this was turning into a complete day-trip, and if she had known that she would have vetoed this idea before the twins knew about it. The knowing look on Sin's face seemed to say he had known exactly how she felt.

'This is coercion, Mr Thornton,' she muttered, glaring her anger at him.

'True,' he agreed unrepentantly.

It was difficult to tell him exactly what she thought of him with the twins so close, but from the way he grinned at her she knew her expression said it all.

Nevertheless, she had still held on to some of her anger by the time they had reached the coastal resort, parked the car, bought buckets and spades for the children, changed into their swimsuits—Andy insisting on going off with Sin to the men's changing room for the latter—before going down on to the beach, Kim and Andy even now down at the water's edge digging for seashells.

'They're loving it,' Sin leant back on his elbows as he watched the children, his bared torso deeply tanned, his navy blue swim trunks only just decent as they revealed the manly shape of him. Robyn had coloured shyly when he first emerged with Andy at his side, and even now she had difficulty looking at his blatant masculinity.

Her own costume wasn't much better, she knew, a one-piece suit from her early married life, not exactly fitted to her fuller breasts. And her blushes had increased as Sin took full inventory of her slender curves, his body reacting in a totally male way, much to her dismay. The twins had been innocently unaware of the sharp sexual tension that suddenly spiced the air between Sin and their mother, chatting happily as they ran on ahead. But Robyn couldn't help but be aware of it, and her skin had tingled as Sin slowly ran his hand down her arm to capture her fingers with his, his grip tight as she would have pulled away. Once again the children saw nothing unusual in their mother holding hands with the tall golden man they were fast coming to adore, and so she had given up any effort of trying to escape, knowing it was futile anyway.

'Weren't they supposed to?' she snapped, at last able to retaliate as she wanted to now that Kim and Andy were out of ear-shot.

He turned to look at her with steady blue eyes. 'I thought we all were.'

Robyn sighed her impatience. 'You aren't playing fair, and you know it.'

'Sorry?' he prompted softly.

'Using the twins to trick me into this day together——'

'Is that what you think I did?' he rasped, his face suddenly hard.

She flushed at his unusual display of anger. 'Well of course it is. You knew Kim and Andy would think you a friend for life for taking them out like this, and after last night you must also know I wouldn't want to come.'

'Last night?' he repeated slowly. 'What happened last night?'

She searched his face in disbelief, meeting only bland enquiry. 'I told you I didn't want you in my life——'

He shook his head. 'You told me you didn't *think* that you did. And I've never been known to give up when there's an element of doubt.'

'There isn't!'

'I happen to think otherwise.'

'I don't *care* what you think, I don't want——'

'Were you always this much of a coward?' he cut in conversationally.

'Coward!' she spluttered her indignation.

Sin nodded. 'With your emotions. Oh I'll admit that you have to be a pretty gutsy lady to have brought up Kim and Andy on your own, but by your own admission they're the only people you feel able to care about.'

'I wish I'd never told you that,' she glared at him fiercely for reminding her of it.

'Maybe you do, but it's too late to retract it now. Can't you see,' he turned on his side, pinning her to the spot on the blanket at his side, the spot they had chosen lay sheltered from the sea-breeze and far enough away from their nearest fellow sun-worshippers to give some degree of privacy, 'that there's no risk involved in loving children, that you can give to them unreservedly and not fear rejection. Loving an adult takes more courage.'

'Love!' she repeated scornfully. 'We aren't talking about love, we're just talking about sex.'

'It's all in the same package between a man and a woman.'

'Rubbish!'

'Maybe to your suppressed little mind it isn't, but——'

'I am not suppressed!' Maybe it was because he had used the same description she herself had used the previous evening that she felt so furiously angry. Whatever the reason she was angrier than she could ever remember being before. 'You're the one who has problems,' she scoffed.

'Me?' his brows rose.

'Yes,' she nodded agitatedly. 'Why else would you need to antagonise a reaction from a woman?'

He looked at her coldly for several long minutes before rising agilely to his feet. 'I think the children could do with a little company,' he said before striding off without so much as a backward glance.

Robyn's gaze followed him frustratedly, knowing that things were in no way resolved between them. And she wanted them resolved, didn't like the hunted feeling he gave her. Hadn't she made her position clear last night? Obviously not. How dare he call her a coward! Was it cowardly not to want an affair with a man who would ultimately walk out on her? But he said he didn't just want an affair with her. What else could he want, he wouldn't be here long enough for them to form any deeper relationship.

And why was she sitting here doing all this soul-searching? She had nothing to reproach herself about, no reason to feel guilty just because she had rejected the man's advances. Sin Thornton had no right to come along and turn her life upside-down in this way!

Once she joined them all at the sea-edge she

made an effort to put her earlier conversation with Sin out of her mind, was determined to enjoy herself for the children's sake. Sin was a little stiff with her to start with, but his easygoing nature precluded him bearing a grudge for any length of time, and by the time they drove home in the early evening, the twins already asleep in the back of the car, the earlier scene on the beach might not have occurred.

'They're lovely children,' Sin told her softly.

She eyed him warily, this the first time they had spoken privately since that last tense conversation. 'Yes,' she agreed guardedly.

'You must be proud of them.'

'I am,' she nodded, wondering where all this was leading to.

'And Brad,' he added hardly, 'is he proud of them too?'

She stiffened at this personal question. 'Of course. Why do you ask?' she questioned tautly.

Sin shrugged. 'Andy happened to mention that he had never been on a beach with his father——'

'*Happened* to mention?' she scoffed angrily. 'It isn't the sort of thing he would "happen" to mention!'

'Meaning I must have prompted him into it?'

'Yes!'

'You're right,' Sin sighed. 'I did.'

'Why?' she frowned.

'I'm not sure,' he admitted huskily.

To Robyn's relief she saw they were almost home. When she had first met Sin yesterday morning she had thought him outrageously flirtatious in a teasing way, and yet each time they talked things became so serious. With Kim and Andy he was a different man entirely, and she wished in a way that she could be included in that light-hearted banter.

'I'll help you carry them inside,' he told her softly after parking in her driveway, the twins not even stirring as he carried first one and then the other into the house and up the stairs to their room.

Robyn eyed him warily across the lounge once she had returned down the stairs, having somehow known he wouldn't take the opportunity to leave while she put the children to bed. 'Thank you for a lovely day,' she said dismissively.

'Kim and Andy enjoyed it,' he finished dryly.

'I did too,' she defended.

Sin shook his head. 'It wasn't the success it should have been.'

Her gaze was unflinching. 'That depends how "successful" you wanted it to be.'

His mouth twisted. 'What a suspicious little mind you do have, Grandma!'

'Years of practice,' she drawled. 'I must have met a dozen men who thought they would be doing me a favour by easing my frustration the last four years.'

'Not me,' he shook his head.

Her brows rose. 'No?'

'I'd be doing me one!' he admitted ruefully, the levity back in his voice. 'I haven't wanted a woman this badly—and known it was so hopeless—since I had a crush on my mother's best friend when I was seventeen.'

Robyn couldn't help smiling at this frank admission. 'Did she know?'

'My mother or her best friend?'

'Either!'

'Mother did,' he nodded. 'Joan didn't notice a

thing. I don't think she could have seen *The Graduate*! I did everything I could think of to make her think of me as a sexually aware young man—all she saw was the young man, with emphasis on the young. It was a terrible blow to my ego,' he grimaced. 'I didn't date for at least a month!'

'Wow!'

'You may laugh, but in those days I thought I was a social outcast if I didn't have a constant stream of girlfriends.'

'*Bed*friends?'

'Yes.'

'And now?'

'Now,' he moved slowly across the room with the grace of a feline, his tread soft and firm, his body fluid. 'Now I know that it's quality rather than quantity.' He took her gently into his arms, moulding the lower half of her body to his as his hands linked at the base of her spine. 'And you, young lady, are quality.'

'Sin——'

His fingertips were gentle on her lips as he silenced her. 'You don't have anything to fear from me, Robyn. I want you, I've admitted I do, but from now on I intend being the "nice man who lives next door".'

'Oh yes,' she scorned with obvious relief, wishing he would release her.

'Think I can't do it?' golden brows rose in challenge.

'It isn't really important——'

'It is to me. I've frightened you today, and I'm usually known as a very nice fellow,' he told her immodestly.

'I'm sure you're very popular,' she mocked to

cover the leaping of her pulse, the weakness in her legs from being this close to him.

'Oh but I am,' Sin nodded in all seriousness, although it was belied by the glitter of humour in his eyes. 'But with you I come on the big heavy, prying into things that don't concern me, antagonising reactions from you,' he added tongue-in-cheek. 'I'm not usually this obvious.'

'So you're going to become a reformed man where I'm concerned?' she taunted.

'Yes.'

It was what she wanted, after all. And she had a feeling this man could be a very good friend.

'Starting tomorrow,' he murmured throatily.

Robyn only just had time to register what he had said before his head lowered and he began to kiss her. She had been unprepared for the intimacy, her body arching up into his of its own volition as she returned the kiss with fervour, knowing that Sin would keep his word as from tomorrow, also knowing that at this moment she didn't care whether he did or didn't.

Desire leapt through Sin's body as she moved sensually against him, and he dragged his mouth away from hers with effort. 'Do you want me to break all my good resolves?' he gasped, a sheen of perspiration to his brow, pale beneath his tan.

She moved away from him as she realised how wantonly she had been behaving. 'I'm sorry——'

'No—don't be sorry.' One long sensitive hand cupped the side of her face. 'But don't repeat it, not if you want me to remain the "nice man who lives next door". I may have more control than I did at seventeen, but my hunger is more intense.'

She couldn't stop the heated wings of colour in her cheeks, moistening her lips nervously, tasting him there, her colour deepening even more as his gaze followed her enjoyment of the movement. 'It's late——'

'And you must be tired,' he nodded, stepping back from her. 'I'm expecting you all to lunch tomorrow, by the way,' he told her as he let himself out.

From the amount of time he was choosing to spend with them she could only presume he meant it when he said Caroline was too young for him. How the other woman was going to love her for that!

CHAPTER FIVE

TRUE to his word Sin did become the 'nice man next door' during the next few days; he also haunted her cottage as if it were his own, even turning up for breakfast one morning after claiming his fridge was empty. Not that she didn't find his company stimulating intellectually, finding they had a lot of things in common, liking the same music and books, having lengthy discussions in the evenings about both.

Only Sin's work remained taboo between them, Sin himself keeping all talk on the subject to a minimum. Which was a pity, because after finding a copy of one of his latest paperbacks in the Colonel's library she had taken it home to read and found that she couldn't put it down until she got to the last page! After all that she had said about his work, and her initial aversion to reading the Colonel's diaries, she was reluctant to admit how wrong she had been. The Colonel obviously had a story to tell from the diaries she had researched so far, and she knew from his writing that Sin was the man to tell it if anyone could.

Caroline was being her usual unreasonable self, still furious with Robyn because of the tours she had to take around every afternoon; as if it had been Robyn's suggestion that she do so! But as far as the younger woman was concerned Sin could do no wrong, her manner always sickeningly sweet whenever he was around. And Sin was around a lot, revelling in the younger woman's attention, humour glittering in his twinkling blue eyes whenever he happened to catch Robyn's gaze. She always looked away whenever he did that, uncomfortable with the feeling that they were sharing a moment of intimacy.

In fact, she was uncomfortable with the whole situation, felt that the twins were coming to rely too much on Sin's company, waiting up in the evenings so that they could spend time with him before going to bed. It would have been petty of her to deny them this treat, and when staying up to see Sin progressed to him helping her put them to bed she couldn't protest at that either, not when it gave the children so much pleasure.

But their growing affection for this likeable man worried her; what would happen when his time here ended and he was gone from all their lives for good? She knew he had to be intelligent enough, sensitive enough, to realise there would be problems when that did happen.

'I'm loyal to my friends, Robyn,' he told her when she mentioned it to him.

It was Thursday evening, and after cooking them all a meal while Sin helped the twins get ready for bed, they were now on their own in the lounge, Kim and Andy settled down for the night. Sin looked relaxed, as he always did, a short-sleeved cream shirt tucked into the low waistband of his denims, his long legs stretched out in front of him as he almost lay in the armchair. Robyn couldn't get over the way he always looked so totally relaxed, sure by the work he produced that he couldn't always be this lazy.

'Even five-year-old ones?' she teased, although there was an underlying edge of seriousness.

His gaze was steady, his mouth unsmiling. 'All my friends,' he told her quietly.

'I know you mean to be kind, Sin——'

'Kindness has never entered into my plans,' he informed her hardly.

'Plans?' She eyed him nervously. 'What plans?'

'Private ones.'

She flushed at the deliberate snub, having become used to the less than serious Sin the last few days, although she knew she probably deserved his coldness; she hadn't liked his interference in her life. But Sin's change in behaviour suddenly made him seem a threat again. 'I didn't mean to pry,' she said stiffly. 'I'm just worried how the twins will react once you leave here.'

'There's nothing to worry about.'

'But——'

'Do you think I would just forget about them once my work here is finished?' There was an angry glitter to his eyes.

'I know you wouldn't mean to be cruel——'

'You're right, I wouldn't,' he bit out, the relaxation gone from his body now as he sat forward in his chair. 'I happen to be very fond of Kim and Andy, I would never do anything that was going to hurt them.'

She sighed, regretting this air of contention between them; she had come to rely on his company a little herself. 'They've grown *too* fond of you.'

'Too fond?' he echoed softly.

'Please don't be offended, Sin,' she pleaded. 'You've been wonderful for them, but——'

'You don't want them to actually love me a little!'

'They love you a lot, that's the trouble!' She was angry too now at his deliberate lack of understanding. 'The three of you have been making plans that can't possibly come true.'

'Name one,' he bit out, his eyes narrowed.

'The skiing trip you were talking of tonight for the new year, for one thing——'

'The twins would love it.'

'But they can't go!'

'I'm not stupid, Robyn, I realise we'll have to fit it in with the school holidays.'

'You're missing my point completely,' she told him frustratedly.

'Maybe because I don't understand the point being made!' he snapped back.

'There won't *be* any holiday in Switzerland!'

Sin became suddenly still, his elbows resting on his splayed knees as he clasped his hands in front of him. 'Why not?' he asked flatly.

She stood up in her agitation, her denims moulded to the length of her legs and hips, the lemon cotton sun-top she wore resting on the waistband of the denims. She looked young and vulnerable at that moment, although she had no idea of that as she faced him across the room. 'I have enough trouble finding the money to take them into town, let alone to Switzerland for skiing holidays!'

'I wouldn't ask you to pay for them——'

'I wouldn't *let* them go any other way!'

'Why the hell not, if I want to take them?' he demanded furiously, his mouth taut.

'Don't you see?' She held up her hands appealingly. 'Kim and Andy already have enough problems adjusting to one part-time father-figure, a second one would be just too much!'

His head snapped back as if she had struck him, uncoiling his long length from the chair as he too stood up. 'That isn't my intention——'

'I know you wouldn't mean it to be like that,' she sighed raggedly. 'But surely you can see that's how it will appear to the twins?'

'Is that how it appears to you?' He didn't answer her question, his eyes narrowed.

'Of course not——'

'Then why the brush-off?'

Her eyes widened. 'I don't know what you mean,' she said slowly, her voice puzzled.

'Of course you do, damn you!' His hands were clenched at his sides. 'Haven't I behaved myself since Saturday?'

'Yes,' she frowned. 'But——'

'Is it because your ex-husband is coming tomorrow? Because I can assure you I have no intention of being difficult about that.'

'Why should you be difficult about Brad wanting to see his children?' she asked dazedly.

'Because he'll also be seeing you,' Sin bit out grimly, his jaw rigid.

Robyn tensed. 'Why should that bother you?' she asked quietly.

'You know why.'

'No, I——'

'Robyn,' he warned softly. 'You *know* why,' he repeated with a firmness that brooked no argument.

Did she? Hadn't she known this past week, that even though he had been acting like a brother or platonic friend where she was concerned, that the attraction beneath them still lurked beneath the surface? Hadn't she known that and shied away from it, as she shied away from it now!

'Sin——'

'You—do—know—why, Robyn,' he said with slow control. 'And because of your nervousness about relationships I've held off pressurising you this last week——'

'*Held off?*' she repeated furiously, glaring up at him. 'You make it sound as if you had a choice!'

'I did,' he nodded confidently, still talking in that controlled voice.

'Like hell you did!' Robyn could never remember being so angry, shaking with it. 'I——' Whatever she had been about to say next was never uttered as one lean hand snaked out about her nape and Sin pulled her up on tiptoe to ruthlessly grind his mouth down on hers, as if pushed to the limit by this heated exchange.

She felt her inner lip split under the pressure, knew the sweet taste of blood in her mouth even as she whimpered her pain. For a brief moment Sin still seemed determined to punish her, then a shudder wracked his body as he fought down his anger, aware of her pain now as the sensuous warmth of his tongue searched the ragged edge of her lip, moving like an erotic balm as deeper emotions than pain engulfed her.

She stopped fighting him as desire possessed her, her body arching up to meet his even as her arms moved about his waist. *This* was what had lurked beneath the surface between them all week, this and all the other wild sensations she had to fight every time she saw him. She told herself she mustn't care about him, certainly not become involved with him, that he was too much like Brad, that beneath his charm he had to be made of the same steel her husband had, that he cared for nothing and no one, and if she did let him close to her he would walk away without a second glance when it suited him to.

She told herself all that, had done so from the moment he had first kissed her, and yet each time he kissed her her resolve weakened. She *wanted* this man, and she knew that he wanted her in return.

Her gasp was caught in his mouth as his hand curved possessively over her breast, bare beneath the cotton sun-top, her nipple surging tautly against his palm, a reaction he had to be aware of.

'Touch me,' she encouraged in a heated groan, knowing she would be devastated by her vocal need when she was alone later tonight. But right now she could only think and feel Sin, forgot everything but him as the buttons were released at the front of her top, the heavy weight of her breast captured in the warmth of his palm, his thumb caressing the throbbing tip.

Sin's mouth moved moistly from her mouth to her throat, caressing each creamy inch of it with slow thoroughness, allowing no respite from knowledgeable hands, holding her breasts now as he massaged them to pert firmness, the throbbing of his thigh evidence of his own need.

Somehow they were no longer standing but pressed close together on the length of the sofa, Sin's thighs partly over hers as his mouth claimed hers in the same erotic rhythm, tasting the nectar to be found there as one of his hands caressed her slowly from breast to thigh, and then back again.

'I knew it would be like this for us,' he murmured achingly as his head lowered and one taut nipple became the captive of the deep cavern of his mouth, the slight tugging movement exciting her even further.

Robyn had known it would be like this too—
and had feared it. They were like two parts of a
whole suddenly finding each other, their bodies
completely enmeshed despite the difference in
their stature, every particle of them attuned to
the other's needs as she ran her hands beneath his
unbuttoned shirt, his skin smooth and slightly
damp to the touch, muscles rippling beneath her
fingertips.

'God, you're lovely!' he groaned raggedly
against her breast. 'Perfect,' he muttered at her
response to him.

She shook her head. 'Not perfect, Sin. I—I have
marks—from when I carried the twins. They——'

His gentle kiss stopped her halting admission.
'They're not something you should ever be
ashamed of,' he assured her. 'They're beautiful.'

'Kim and Andy . . .?'

He nodded. 'And the changes in your body
that gave you them.' His eyes darkened to navy as
he looked down at her. 'I wish I could have been
their father!'

Robyn stiffened in his arms. 'Sin . . .?'

'Oh don't worry,' he gave a harsh laugh. 'I'm
not eaten up with jealousy because you had
another man's children, that happened long
before I met you.' His arms tightened about her
painfully. 'But if you became involved with
another man now it would be a different matter.'

'Another man?'

His eyes were as hard as the bright jewels they
resembled. 'Yes!'

'You mean Brad?' Something in his expression
told her that was exactly who he meant!

Sin drew in a ragged breath. 'You never did
tell me how you felt about seeing him tomorrow.'

Robyn was still beneath him, suddenly finding his weight intolerable. 'I told you how I felt about my marriage,' she reminded him stiffly.

'That was years ago——'

'Brad hasn't changed——'

'But you have,' Sin grated. 'You've matured, grown up.'

'Not that much.' She pushed past him and stood up, her hands shaking as she rebuttoned her top. 'I think you had better go,' her voice trembled with emotion, suppressed anger mainly, although there was some hurt there too.

'Robyn——'

'Before I say something we'll both regret,' she finished between tight lips.

Sin watched her between narrowed lids, making no effort to rebutton his own clothing, his chest darkly golden. 'Say it,' he invited softly.

Her mouth tightened. 'I don't think there's any need to, I'm sure you're well aware of my feelings. Now would you please leave.'

He stood up in lithe movements. 'If you have nothing to say then I do,' he grated. 'I know what you thought was going to happen here tonight——'

'What do you mean?' she demanded sharply, her face suddenly pale.

'You wanted to go to bed with me——'

'No!' her protest came out as a strangulated cry.

'You wanted to go to bed with me,' he repeated hardly. 'But only on your terms. And no matter how aroused I may have seemed to you just now I would never have let it go that far.'

'The experience of your added maturity?' she was stung into replying.

The quirk to his mouth was completely devoid

of humour as he shook his head. 'The need for a real response from you——'

'And what happened just now wasn't *real?*' she accused in heated disbelief.

'It was very real,' he nodded. 'In a physical sense. Did your mind even acknowledge I was the man making love to you?'

Robyn's face was ashen now, her gasp pained. 'Of course I knew it was you!'

'Did you?' he derided bitterly. 'I don't think so. But don't think I'm going to make any of this easier for you,' he warned grimly. 'If I had made love to you just now you would have been able to console yourself with the fact that I had seduced you, that you had no choice. What you want from me is a no risk affair, a brief sexual encounter where you don't have to be involved in any other way. But before I've finished with you, you'll be involved right up to your beautiful neck,' he promised harshly.

'You're insane! I have no idea what you're talking about——'

'Oh, you know, Robyn,' he contradicted softly. 'You just aren't willing to admit it yet, to yourself or me. But just remember that I'm the one you want when you see your ex-husband tomorrow. I would hate you to mistake the feelings I'm arousing as a renewed desire for him,' the threat in his voice couldn't be mistaken for anything else.

'That's a disgusting thing to say!'

He shook his head. 'That's a fact of life. And with him you definitely know there would be no more involved than a night of sex.'

Her mouth turned back with distaste. 'You and Caroline have the same disgusting minds.'

'If she realised the same thing could happen then we have more in common than I first thought.'

'Are you sure you wouldn't rather have an affair with her?' she scorned.

'I'm not going to have an affair with anyone,' Sin told her hardly. 'And I'm warning you now that you hadn't better either.'

'Warning me?' this time her gasp was of outrage. 'You have no right to warn me about anything! How dare you threaten me?'

'When an animal is being cornered it turns and attacks,' he told her calmly. 'Take care, Robyn, because that's exactly what you're doing.' He walked over to the door. 'And when I attack back you'll know that you've lost.'

The room was suddenly empty as he left, the cottage door closing softly seconds later. And in the ensuing minutes Robyn realised that the strange noise she could hear was her own choked sobbing.

'What have you done to yourself?'

Robyn bristled at Brad's greeting comment as she opened the cottage door to him. What she had 'done' was newly wash her hair, blow-drying it into a soft style about her face and shoulders, apply a light make-up, and put on a black ruffled blouse and fitted black trousers, the latter emphasising every curve of her body. She had been rather pleased at how coolly sophisticated she looked when she viewed her reflection in her bedroom mirror, and within seconds Brad had completely stripped her confidence from her.

She followed him through to the lounge as he strode confidently through the cottage, unmoved by the way he exuded a lambent sensuality in the close-fitting blue trousers and lighter blue shirt, the latter unbuttoned down his chest, its colour adding a warmth to assessing grey eyes that wasn't normally there. At thirty-four Brad was still everything that was tall, dark and handsome, although there was a ruthlessness about him now, and the lines beside his nose and mouth weren't from laughter, the grey hair among the thick darkness seeming more abundant than it had several months ago.

'If you've come here to be insulting, Brad——'

'I wasn't being in the least insulting,' he drawled, eyeing her speculatively. 'You look good, really good, better than I've ever seen you. That wouldn't have anything to do with the man who answered the telephone last week, would it?' he mocked.

Robyn blushed in spite of herself, knowing how guilty that must make her look. 'Nothing at all,' she snapped.

'You never did tell me who he was.'

'Because it's none of your business!'

'I've never tried to keep from you the identity of the current woman in my life,' he drawled.

'I've never asked.' She had never needed to, Brad seeming to find pleasure in relating his different relationships to her; she knew the most recent was a woman called Tina.

The smile he gave taunted as well as insulted. 'I thought you might be interested in what you were missing—although it seems you're no longer missing out on it. My dear cousin is spitting venom over the fact that you seem to be making a fool of yourself over one of Henry's guests.'

'Your dear cousin happens to be as jealous as
hell!'

Grey eyes narrowed at her uncharacteristic
outburst. 'Now you really do have me intrigued,'
Brad said slowly.

'Why?' she asked guardedly.

'Normally only defence of the twins brings out
this fierce streak in you, but it seems Sin
Thornton can do the same thing,' he speculated.

She had wondered if he actually knew the
identity of his uncle's guest, had deliberately not
mentioned his name herself in the hope of
avoiding bringing personalities into this senseless
conversation. She should have known that Brad
was just playing one of his games with her, that
he had been aware Sin was the man staying next
door all along.

'I was defending myself, not him,' she bit out
abruptly.

'I don't believe you.'

The colour deepened in her cheeks. 'I don't
give a damn whether you believe me or not, I
don't have to explain myself or my actions to you
any more. You——'

'Where are Kim and Andy?' he interrupted
calmly.

Robyn drew in a steadying breath, knowing
Brad was satisfied now that he had managed to
anger her; he and Caroline both had that
malicious streak in them. 'They're upstairs
getting ready for bed. It's after eight, and——'

'I told you not to pin me down to a time,' he
reminded hardly.

'And I haven't,' she bit out. 'I fed the twins at
their usual time, I just thought it would be better
if they were in their nightclothes when you

arrived so that they wouldn't be too late to bed. They're excited enough about tomorrow as it is!'

'Tomorrow? Oh you mean the trip to London,' he dismissed uninterestedly.

'They've never been there before,' she snapped.

He shrugged. 'It's no big deal.'

'They don't know that. Brad, you will——'

'Daddy!' Two childishly excited voices cried out in unison before Kim and Andy launched themselves across the room and into their father's waiting arms.

Robyn watched her children's obvious adoration of their father with a melting heart, her probing as to why Brad had suddenly decided they should visit his home forgotten in the hour of excitement that followed his arrival. He may ignore the twins' existence for months at a time, may make his visits and telephone calls as brief as possible, but she couldn't dispute the fact that he *did* make the effort to see them. And feeling about children as she knew he did she had to silently thank him for that.

'Alone at last,' he mocked once the children were in bed.

Robyn served the steak, salad, and baked potatoes she had prepared for their meal, refusing to rise to his taunt. 'What time will you be leaving in the morning?' she prompted.

He shrugged. 'About ten, I suppose. Don't worry, Robyn, your babies will be perfectly safe with me,' he taunted at her worried expression.

'They're your babies too!' she flashed, the delicious food suddenly losing its appeal.

'Oh I've never disputed that, I know I satisfied you enough in bed when we first married for you not to have taken a lover after only two months.' He sat back in his chair, sipping his wine, unmoved by the outrage in her face. 'Is Sin satisfying you now?'

The question took her offguard, and she almost choked on her food.

'It's quite convenient for you him having the adjoining cottage,' Brad's brows rose challengingly.

'He needed the privacy for his work!'

'But does his bed there ever get used?' Brad drawled mockingly.

'Don't attribute everyone with your own morals,' she snapped furiously.

'You mean he doesn't sleep here?'

'Of course not! Even supposing I were interested in that sort of relationship with him, which I'm not,' she added a little too vehemently, 'you don't seriously think I would risk the twins finding me in bed with him here, do you?'

'No, I suppose not,' he conceded thoughtfully. 'But he is round here a lot, isn't he?'

Once again her blushes gave her away. 'The twins like him.'

'And they're in bed by seven-thirty.'

'I like him too,' she stated challengingly. 'He's very stimulating company.'

'I heard that,' Brad derided.

Robyn stiffened at the amusement in his voice. 'What did you hear?'

'When Sin was still reporting it was reputed that he more than earned that shortened version of his name with the ladies. Love them and leave them doesn't begin to describe it,' Brad taunted dryly.

'And now?'

He shrugged. 'Who knows? But I doubt he's changed that much.'

She doubted it too, knew from his own behaviour with her that Sin wanted to make love to her, that he may even be making love to Caroline tonight; she had heard him go out shortly before Brad arrived, and Caroline had gloatingly informed her earlier today that Sin was going up to the main house for dinner tonight. She hadn't seen him herself since last night, had no idea if they were still friends. She had a feeling it would be better for everyone if they weren't!

'You know,' Brad said slowly, 'you look better than just good, there's something about you now that wasn't there when I was married to you. I don't suppose, since you say you don't sleep with Thornton, that you would consider letting me share your bed tonight?'

'No!' she told him in a bewildered voice. What was *wrong* with everyone all of a sudden? Four years she and Brad had been separated, and not once during that time had he shown the slightest attraction to her, let alone wanting to go to bed with her. She would have been stunned with surprise if she had known it was her own awakening sensuality that made everyone else's actions seem so out of character to her, that they were just reacting to her.

'I thought not,' Brad didn't press the subject of staying with her, standing up to leave. 'I'd better be going, I should spend some time with Henry before I leave. How is the book going, do you know?'

'Why should I?'

'Don't be so aggressive, Robyn, it isn't

attractive in a woman.' He tapped her cheek playfully, his smile becoming cruel as she flinched away from him. 'Henry mentioned you were helping Thornton with his research,' he answered her question in a hard voice.

She nodded abruptly. 'As far as I know it's going well.'

She was silent as she walked to the door with him, still shaken by his proposition, unaware of the changes in herself, of the needs of her body, of the slumbering passion in the depths of her eyes. But the man at her side was aware of it all, and he knew it wasn't for him, that whether she knew it or not it was Sin Thornton she wanted.

'Robyn, I——' Brad broke off what he had been going to say as the sound of a powerful car approaching the cottages could be heard coming down the road, mocking satisfaction gleaming in cold grey eyes as he pulled Robyn into his arms, his mouth capturing hers.

Robyn was too stunned by the unexpected action to offer more than a token protest, her mouth numb beneath Brad's as he continued to kiss her as the powerful headlights of the Porsche outlined them in the darkness and the car was turned into the neighbouring driveway, Sin behind the wheel.

CHAPTER SIX

As she pulled furiously out of Brad's arms she heard the powerful engine die away, immediately followed by the slamming of the car door. She turned back to Brad with blazing eyes. 'You did that deliberately!'

'Yes.'

'*Why?*'

His expression was calmly thoughtful. 'To see how you would react,' he told her.

'I've already said no,' she snapped, wiping the touch of his mouth from her lips with trembling fingertips.

'Oh, not your reaction to that, Robyn,' he mocked hardly, his eyes taking on a dangerous glitter as he watched her action. 'I wanted to see how you would feel about Thornton seeing you kissing me.'

The colour came and went in her face in rapid succession, leaving her deathly pale. 'I wasn't kissing you!'

Brad shrugged. 'He couldn't tell who was kissing who from that distance.'

She felt sick at this cruel manipulation, although it was something she should have expected from Brad; at the end of their marriage he had taken fiendish delight in forcing her physically to his will when he knew the sexual act held no pleasure for her so soon after the twins were born. She had pleaded with him to be patient, had explained that many women felt the same way after giving birth, that with patience and gentleness she would once again be an active participant in their sex-life. Brad hadn't given her either, didn't have time for such things, and had demanded what he called his 'conjugal rights'. His abuse of her then made it impossible for her to feel anything but loathing for any physical contact between them now. And she despised him utterly for treating her that way in front of a man whose respect she valued.

'Your face tells me a lot,' Brad taunted.

'Does it tell you how much I dislike you?' she spat the words at him.

His mouth twisted. 'I already knew that. I'm well aware of the fact that you only keep up appearances between us for the sake of the children.'

'And what's your excuse?'

'I don't have one,' he shook his head. 'I've always liked you, Robyn—I should just never have married you,' he added dryly.

'Then why did you?'

He shrugged. 'I wanted you. And maybe—just for a time—I thought it would be nice to have someone to come home to.' His mouth hardened. 'I never thought you would be stupid enough to get pregnant straight away!'

She didn't even flinch at the accusation, had heard it too many times in the past to be affected by it; as if the twins' conception had somehow been achieved without his enthusiastic help!

'I'm sure you aren't naive enough to make the same mistake with Thornton,' he added nastily.

'I told you, we aren't sleeping together!'

His smile mocked her. 'I didn't for one moment think you would be "sleeping".'

She gave a weary sigh. 'We aren't doing anything else either.'

'Then why did you look so upset at the thought of him seeing us together just now?'

It was useless to deny that she had been upset, but she could no more answer Brad than she could answer herself. It was no good telling herself she simply hadn't liked being made to look a liar, it wasn't that that made her feel so ashamed.

'We're divorced——'

'We could have made a mistake.'

'We didn't.'

'No,' Brad acknowledged softly. 'You've matured, Robyn, but living with you would still drive me insane. The thought of going through that "domestic bliss" for a second time fills me with the shudders!'

'Don't worry,' her mouth twisted. 'I doubt you'll ever have to suffer it again.'

'You never know,' he shrugged. 'Stranger things have been known to happen.'

'Not this time,' she scorned.

Brad looked at her with admiring eyes. 'You know, if it wouldn't cause too many complications I really would have liked an affair with you.'

'Then aren't I lucky those complications exist!'

He was still chuckling as he strode over to his car, pausing after opening the door. 'Thanks for tonight, Robyn,' he called slightly louder than was necessary, glancing pointedly over at the blazing lights in every room in the adjoining cottage as he did so. 'I enjoyed our time together—as usual,' he added huskily, his mocking humour increasing at her furiously angry expression.

The innuendo behind his words couldn't be mistaken for anything else, and after watching him depart Robyn closed the door behind her with suppressed anger.

But why should it matter so much what Sinclair Thornton thought of her? Why did she have this overwhelming urge to run over to the neighbouring cottage and explain exactly what he had seen and heard?

It was a desire she resisted as confusion swept over her. Since last night, since Sin had threatened her so subtly she had tried not to think about him or her own feelings towards him. If she had any feelings towards him. Oh, he had the power to induce in her a desire long lain dormant, gave her pleasure where at the end Brad hadn't cared whether she had pleasure or not, had in fact seemed to enjoy punishing her for being his wife. Maybe it was just Sin's gentleness with her that made her want to defend what he had just seen, because it certainly wasn't love. She wasn't stupid enough to mistake desire and liking for love a second time!

And she couldn't just go over to Sin's cottage at this time of night to tell him her husband's kiss and subsequent derisive comment had meant nothing to her. That would be assuming that Sin felt more for her than a fleeting attraction, and no matter how kind he was to her, or how good he was to the children, she daren't assume anything where he was concerned.

She was only halfway up the stairs on her way to bed when she heard the sound of the powerful engine of the Porsche leap back into life once again, running the rest of the way to the top of the stairs to look out of the window there, just in time to see the car backing out of the driveway, the dark interior making it impossible for her to see Sin's face as he accelerated the car away with a screech of tyres.

She had no idea where he could be going this time of night, but she didn't think she was assuming anything by guessing the reason for his going; Brad's behaviour had had the desired effect. And after she had told Sin she wasn't interested in her ex-husband! The thought of what Sin must now think of her made her feel sick, making her realise once again how much she had come to value his respect. And no matter how deeply she might respond to him, her surrender the previous evening total, she knew that until a few moments ago she had had Sin's respect.

By the time she had washed and changed into her nightgown, tried to interest herself in a book that in her agitation made no sense to her, she still hadn't heard the Porsche return. Where could Sin have gone? The first thought that came to her mind was Caroline, but she quickly dismissed that; Sin could hardly spend the night with the younger woman under her father's roof!

But he still hadn't returned to the cottage when she finally drifted off to sleep shortly after two, and when she awoke with a start just before six the first thing she did was get out of bed and go to the window; the neighbouring driveway was empty. Sin hadn't returned to the cottage all night!

After her almost sleepless night the last thing she felt in the mood for was Kim and Andy's exuberance over their visit to London, their excitement barely containable. By the time Brad arrived to collect them her head was pounding and she had managed to snap at both the children at least twice, an unusual occurrence at any time, let alone when they were going away from her for the first time in their young lives.

'I'll take care of them,' Brad assured her mockingly as she kept glancing over to where the twins were already ensconced in the back of Brad's car, the two of them talking on the pathway.

'Kim has a slight cold so keep an eye on her, and Andy——'

'You've already told me about them a dozen times,' he interrupted wearily.

'I know, but Kim likes to put a brave face on things when she feels ill, and——'

'Robyn!' Brad's impatience was barely contained. 'It's only overnight, I doubt she'll deteriorate to an asthmatic attack.'

She was aware that she was panicking over what was merely a snuffly nose, but now that the time had come for Kim and Andy to leave she just wanted to snatch them back into the house and tell Brad he couldn't have them, not even for thirty-six hours. Which was completely selfish of her when the children couldn't wait to be on their way.

'I'm sure you'll realise if she gets any worse,' she conceded quietly.

'I'm sure,' he nodded, glancing over at the neighbouring cottage. 'Your neighbour is out bright and early this morning.'

Robyn stiffened at his questioning tone. 'Yes.'

'Argued, have you?' Brad mocked her sudden withdrawal.

She met his gaze with unflinching brown eyes.

'Considering I haven't seen Sin since we saw him together last night that would be a little difficult.'

His mouth quirked. 'Giving you the silent treatment, is he?' he mused.

'Don't be ridiculous,' she snapped. 'Sin wouldn't stoop to such things.'

'Beneath his dignity, is it?'

'Yes!'

'Don't be a fool, Robyn,' Brad derided. 'If it will get a woman into his bed a man will use any ploy.'

'Sin is merely *out*, Brad,' she told him curtly. 'Not playing stupid games.'

'Talking of games,' he drawled, 'I don't think Caroline would be averse to playing a few games with him if you aren't interested.'

Her mouth turned back with distaste for his crudeness. 'Caroline can do as she chooses.'

'She usually does,' he said with amusement. 'She's gone off to London this morning and left Henry in the lurch with half-a-dozen planned tours. Perhaps you ought to go and help him out as you have nothing better to do now that the twins are going with me.'

It wasn't his arrogant assumption that he could still tell her what to do and when to do it that shook her, it was the fact that Caroline had left so abruptly for London. London. Could that be where Sin had gone too, after all it was his home? Surely it had to be too much of a coincidence for them both to have taken off so suddenly. Perhaps the meeting had been pre-arranged, maybe she *had* been arrogant in assuming Sin had left so abruptly last night because he had seen her with Brad!

'Robyn?' Brad prompted impatiently at her preoccupation.

'I—Yes, I'll go up to the house later,' she only just managed to recall the last thing he had said to her, angry with herself for her erroneous assumption.

'I should,' he nodded. 'After all, we mustn't upset old Henry, must we?'

'Mustn't we?' she answered vaguely.

'Not when I'm the only male heir he has,' Brad snapped, as if her stupidity in not realising that amazed him.

Robyn looked at him with puzzled eyes. 'You surely aren't expecting anything from him when he dies?'

'Why not?'

'Because——'

'Look, I have to go, Robyn,' he cut in abruptly. 'Before the twins wreck the inside of my car.' He glared over to where the two children were looking interestedly at the workings of the car.

She stiffened at his criticism. 'They're just excited,' she defended.

'Excited enough to crash the damn car into your wall if I don't get in there soon,' he nodded grimly. 'I'll see you tomorrow, Robyn,' he called over his shoulder as he strode to the car. 'And I have no idea what time it will be,' he derisively answered her next question before she asked it. 'I'll telephone you once we've arrived, if I think of it.'

Robyn knew he wouldn't think of it, but as she had his telephone number she intended calling herself when a suitable time had elapsed for them to have arrived.

She stood in the driveway and waved them off, standing there until she could no longer see the excited faces of the twins pressed against the back window, desolation sweeping over her as she turned to go back into the house. She was used to the twins being at school all day, had even allowed them to spend the day with friends at weekends in the past, but she had never before known this complete separation from them, a separation that stretched intolerably before her.

Her whole life had revolved around Kim and Andy since the moment they were born, even more so after Brad had gone, and she simply didn't know how to fill her time without them. Maybe she should go up to the main house and help the Colonel out after all; she had nothing else to do.

She felt as if she were escaping when she hurried from the cottage fifteen minutes later, wearing one of the smart blouses and fitted skirts that was her usual uniform when she went to work. As Brad had predicted, Caroline had left behind her complete chaos, the rest of the morning and afternoon passing so quickly Robyn didn't have time to brood about the twins' absence, only just making time to call Brad's apartment later that morning, the conversation necessarily short as he was taking the children out shopping.

Being so busy all day also stopped her thinking about Sin, and the fact that Caroline was probably in London with him right now. Although she didn't have the same success when she finally got back to the cottage after six to find the Porsche—and Sin—were still conspicuous in their absence. She felt more alone than ever knowing Sin wasn't there, and to think of him

with Caroline . . .! It was useless to deny that that
bothered her, because it bothered her a lot.

The thought of sitting down to a solitary
dinner suddenly brought the whole world
crashing down around her, hating the fact that
the twins were away, hating even more the fact
that Sin was with Caroline when she needed him
so much. She mentally recoiled from the
admission even as she recognised it, feeling the
tears begin to fall down her cheeks. She knew she
was falling apart emotionally, and there was just
nothing she could do to stop it.

'What the———! Robyn, what's going on?'

She looked up at the sound of that harshly
grating voice, not caring how he came to be there
as she stood up to run into Sin's waiting arms.
'Sin!' she sobbed her relief as she felt his strong
arms move reassuringly about her.

'What is it?' he demanded into her hair. 'Has
someone hurt you?'

She shook her head, feeling safe and secure
with her face buried against his throat, intoxicated
by the smell of his aftershave, and the much more
basically male smell that was all Sin.

'Your ex-husband . . .?'

'He isn't here,' she shook her head again, her
voice muffled. 'He's gone back to London.'

Sin's arms tightened painfully about her
slender waist. 'Is that why you're crying?'

'Of course not.'

'Then why . . .?'

'He's taken the twins with him!' She began to
cry again, seeming unable to stop now that she
had started.

Sin pulled back to look down at her with
concerned eyes. 'Brad took the twins away from

you?' he rasped angrily.

She realised from his fury that he had misunderstood her. 'No, no,' she hastened to explain. 'He's just taken them for a visit. And you were gone too——'

'I've been up to London——'

Even as she realised that she began to pull away, remembering that Caroline had gone there too. 'I know,' she said frostily.

'You do?' Sin sounded puzzled.

'Yes.' She stood away from him, regretting her moment of weakness. She may be feeling the loneliest she had ever been, but that was no reason to cry all over a man she would be better to avoid all contact with.

Sin thrust his hands into the back pockets of his faded denims, the action pulling the bottle-green short-sleeved shirt he wore taut across his muscled chest. 'How did you know?' he frowned.

She turned away. 'Caroline left for there early this morning, and——'

'And you think I've been with her?' He spun her around angrily, a dark flush to his cheeks. 'You know damn well why I left here last night—and it had nothing to do with Caroline Masters!' he bit out tautly.

'Are you saying you haven't been with her today?' she said disbelievingly.

'I'm saying that after last night I'm not sure it's any of your business!'

Deep colour heightened her cheeks as she knew she probably deserved the accusation, how could she act jealously when last night he had seen her, to all intents and purposes, in her ex-husband's arms? How could she act jealous at all when she kept denying, to herself as well as to him, that she wanted a relationship with him?

'Or is it?' Sin asked slowly as he saw the confusion in her expression.

She swallowed hard, blushing as she looked up at him. What did she want from this man, did she want anything? She hadn't thought she had, but suddenly she wanted him to know exactly what he had seen the previous evening. 'It was Brad's idea of a joke,' she told him tiredly.

'A joke?'

She nodded in the face of his disbelief. 'He has a warped sense of humour.'

'He would have to have to have found that in the least funny!' Sin growled.

She could see that he still didn't believe her, and suddenly it was imperative that he did. 'We had been arguing most of the evening, about you mainly.' She evaded his gaze as she saw the sudden interest there. 'And when he heard you coming home he decided to cause a little mischief.'

'Mischief!' Sin snorted disgustedly. 'I left here last night with murder in my mind.'

'Mine?'

'His! I heard him leave and I wondered if it were just for appearances sake, if he would be coming back later. And if he did I didn't want to be here,' he added grimly.

'He didn't come back, Sin,' she told him with simple honesty, her gaze frank.

Sin's eyes were narrowed as he remained unconvinced. 'He doesn't want you?'

'I don't know what he wants, and I don't particularly care,' she avoided his gaze, unsure any more *what* Brad wanted. 'But I *am* sure what

I want,' she had no trouble looking at Sin now. 'I don't want him.'

'And me?' he queried softly. 'Do you want me?'

She swallowed, drawing in a steadying breath. 'That's something else I'm *not* sure of . . .'

Some of the tension seemed to leave him as a wide grin lightened his features. 'Even that's an improvement.'

'It is,' she frowned.

'Of course,' he nodded, looking pleased with himself—and more like the Sin she had first met. 'I came over to see if you and the twins would like to join me for dinner tonight, but in their absence the invitation to you still stands.'

She hesitated about accepting, aware that the presence of the twins had acted as a sort of defence against Sin's attraction to her, that the thought of being completely alone with him made her nervously aware of her own vulnerability where he was concerned.

'I'm cooking,' he encouraged softly.

'That will make a change,' she teasingly fell in with the game he was playing.

'Wait until you've tried my cooking.'

'The Sunday lunch you cooked was good. What would you be having tonight?'

'Duck. With orange sauce. And——'

'All right, you've talked me into it,' she smiled.

'The way to a woman's heart is through her stomach,' he quipped dryly.

'This woman's it is,' she nodded. 'I've been cooking for you all week.'

'Would you rather go out for a meal?' he frowned as the thought occurred to him. 'The duck will keep.'

She wasn't really in the mood to sit in a formal restaurant, would much rather spend the evening quietly with Sin, would still be able to hear her telephone if it rang, worried in case the twins should need her. 'The duck sounds wonderful,' she answered Sin. 'Although I would like to change before we eat.' She looked down ruefully at her slightly creased skirt and blouse.

He nodded agreement of that. 'Dinner won't be ready for a while anyway. Just come over when you're ready, hmm?'

'Fine. I—About last night . . .' She was aware that nothing had been settled between them about that.

Some of the humour left Sin's face, leaving it hard and uncompromising. 'If you say nothing happened with your ex-husband then I believe you.'

'Nothing happened. And Caroline?' It was strangely imperative that there be honesty between them.

He shrugged broad shoulders. 'Whoever she went to London to see it wasn't me.'

'I'll be over in half an hour,' she told him softly.

There was an unfamiliar air of excitement about her as she changed into the black gown, knowing that the clinging style hadn't dated in the six years she had had the dress, that the snug-fitting material clearly claimed she wasn't the young girl Sin had first thought her, but a mature woman. Her hair she brushed loosely about her shoulders, her make-up heavier than usual, her eyeshadow brown, her long lashes made to look even longer with the application of mascara, her lipgloss a deep burnt orange. A quick spray of her favourite perfume and she felt more than ready for her evening with Sin, knew that her relationship with him was going to change before the night was over.

Sin had changed too when he opened the door to her, his black shirt the finest silk, his black trousers moulded to the lean length of legs and thighs, his hair still slightly damp after a shower. He was tall and virile, and Robyn's senses lurched at the sight of him.

'Just in time for a drink.' He handed her one of the glasses of wine he had just poured. 'Now that you're here I'll put the duck in the oven.'

Robyn watched in amazement as he took a silver-foil manufacturer's tray out of the re- frigerator and put it in the oven. 'I thought you said you were cooking?'

'I am,' he nodded, putting a similar carton of cooked vegetables in beside the duck.

'That's cheating,' she gasped incredulously, beginning to laugh.

Sin gave her a look of feigned innocence. 'I can assure you it's very good. Sunday's lunch came out of similar cartons.'

She knew the brand name on the cartons, knew the food was of good quality, but even so——!

'Wait until you try it,' Sin told her confidently. 'It beats slaving over a hot stove any day.'

She had to admit that the duck melted in her mouth when it was served to her, the orange sauce delicious, the whole meal—although coming from a seemingly endless stream of boxes and tins—was mouth-watering.

'So tell me,' Sin prompted as they lingered over eating the strawberry cheesecake. 'How often does Brad take the twins off like this?'

Some of the enjoyment went out of the evening for her as she was reminded of her children's absence. 'Never before,' she told him softly.

'Isn't it a little odd that he should do so now?' he frowned.

'Yes.'

'Which is why you were so preoccupied when he called last week,' Sin suddenly realised.

'Yes,' she said again, more flatly this time.

'I'm sure they will be all right with him, Robyn.' His hand moved to cover hers.

'I'm sure they will too,' she nodded. 'I just——' her bottom lip quivered precariously as she tried to control her tears—and failed. 'I'm sorry to be so silly about this,' she looked about her frantically for a handkerchief as the tears fell in earnest.

'You're just being a mother,' Sin told her gently, standing up to come round the table and pull her up into his arms. 'Robyn——'

'Hold me, Sin,' she choked as she turned into him. 'Please hold me!'

'God, yes!' His arms tightened convulsively, the gentleness replaced by burning desire. 'I promised myself I wouldn't do this,' he groaned, his face contorted with passion. 'But I need you.'

'I need you too,' she admitted raggedly, her face raised to his as she received his bruising kiss.

In Sin's arms, with his mouth and hands working a dizzying magic over her body, she could forget her unhappiness, could think and feel only him, groaning her need as his mouth left hers to travel the length of her throat.

'I *need* you,' she repeated more forcefully.

He raised his head to look down at her, dark blue eyes searching the anguished desire in her face before he took her hand and led the way up the stairs to his bedroom.

CHAPTER SEVEN

'No,' she halted his hand as he would have put on all the lights.

Sin's gaze held hers as he gently but firmly removed her hand. 'There's going to be nothing furtive or illicit about our making love,' he ground out, the lights blazing. 'I'm not ashamed of needing to make love to you, and you shouldn't be ashamed of the way you feel either.'

'I'm not,' she shook her head.

'Then why——'

'I'm shy,' she explained pleadingly. 'Just shy,' she repeated huskily. 'I've only ever been with one man——'

'And I doubt that he appreciated you as you should be appreciated,' Sin rasped.

'Until I became big with the twins he did,' she recalled honestly. 'Then he changed.'

'I don't want to hear about Brad or your marriage to him,' he cut in harshly. 'You're with me now, Robyn.'

He gave her no chance to explain further about Brad and herself, kissing her with fierceness even as his hand moved to switch out the overhead light, leaving only the glow of the bedside lamp. Robyn relaxed in his arms at his unspoken understanding, feeling the angry tension leaving his body as with a groan his mouth began to devour hers, tasting and gently biting until only their ragged breathing could be heard in the stillness of the room.

Sin's mouth didn't leave hers as he expertly removed the clinging black dress, leaving her clothed only in peach-coloured bra and panties, his hands causing shock-waves of pleasure through her body, shivering with reaction as the fullness of her breast was suddenly bared to his questing lips.

'I think,' he said with husky softness, 'that I might be at less of a disadvantage if we were on the bed,' he gently mocked the disparity of their heights.

Giving him a shy smile she took his hand and led him over to the wide double bed, stopping at its side. 'Shouldn't you undress first?'

'You undress me,' he invited.

Hot colour entered her cheeks. 'I'm not sure I know how,' she admitted gruffly. Brad may like to think of himself as a liberated man, but as husband and wife they had only ever made love beneath the privacy of their bedclothes.

'Try,' Sin encouraged softly.

Her movements were hesitant at first, then all the more knowledgeable as she sensed Sin's efforts to maintain control, his breathing shallow as she slipped his shirt from his shoulders, his jaw rigid with tension as she kissed his hardened nipples, his hands clenched at his sides as she glanced up at him with a smile of satisfaction. She was filled with confidence at his unhidden reaction to her caresses, her hands moving lower.

'No!' he stopped her, the blaze in his eyes almost out of control.

'Please.' Her eyes were like liquid gold as she pleaded up at him.

Desire warred with necessity, until finally necessity won. 'I want this to last, Robyn,' he

told her gruffly as he put her away from him.
'And if I let you touch me any more now it will
all be over before it's begun.' He chuckled at the
blush in her cheeks. 'It isn't easy to admit that
you make me feel like an adolescent!'

Her confidence restored she gave a throaty
laugh as she sat back on the bed. 'In that case I'll
just watch the floor-show!' she teased him.

'Wanton!' he growled as he quickly divested
himself of the last of his clothing.

Robyn felt her pulse rate leap as she gazed at
the golden nakedness of his body, the broad
shoulders and chest tapering down to a narrow
waist, his thighs taut with desire, long legs
firmly muscled. The hair that covered most of his
body was slightly darker than that on his head,
although it still gleamed golden.

The bed dipped slightly as he joined her there,
their mouths fusing in heated passion as they
caressed each other with searching hands, Robyn
gasping as Sin's palm warmly cupped her
womanhood through the lace briefs she still
wore, feeling the instant flood of emotion there.

'Did you like what you saw?' Sin encouraged
her verbal lovemaking before taking the dark
peak of one breast into his mouth, his tongue
flicking sensuously over its hardness before
giving its twin the same consideration.

Her answer was to tentatively touch what she
had seen, her caressing fingers telling of the
pleasure she found in his male beauty, feeling
him instantly harden and strengthen against her
caress.

'Tell me what else you like,' he urged raggedly.
'Show me, Robyn!'

During the next few minutes they discovered

each other's pleasure spots with unerring accuracy, Robyn at last pleading for his possession of her, as naked as he now, the moist heat between her thighs telling her she was ready for him.

She gasped out loud as they merged together, Sin filling her completely, utterly, spasms of ecstasy claiming her body as he slowly began to move inside her, his face taut with desire as she looked up at him, clinging to his shoulders as the world seemed to sway beneath her.

The final ecstasy, when it came, shook her to the very depths of her being, her nails digging into the flesh of his buttocks as she felt him tauten and go over the edge with her, the hoarse groan he gave one of immense and satisfying triumph.

Robyn breathed in the intoxicating smell of him as they lay still, a part of him as they rested, Sin's chest heaving above her before he gave a shuddering sigh and buried his face in her throat.

'I hope a night without sleep won't be too much of a strain for you?' he teased later, a satisfied curve to his mouth.

They didn't go completely without sleep, the short naps they had between increasingly passionate lovemaking more than enough to sustain them, the magic times in Sin's arms more than enough to convince her she was no longer averse to physical love.

The sun was shining brightly when she at last emerged from beneath the bedclothes, blinking tiredly to focus on reserved blue eyes, Sin lying at her side, the dark blond growth of beard on his chin evidence that he hadn't been up yet either, despite the obvious lateness of the hour.

It was the reserve in his eyes that held her back from throwing her arms about his neck and telling him how wonderful she thought he was.

He continued to look at her silently for several more tense minutes. 'Now is your cue to tell me that last night was a mistake, that you acted impulsively, that it was because you were so upset about the twins that you allowed yourself to be seduced into my bed,' his voice was flat, emotionless.

'You forgot "I had too much wine and didn't know what I was doing",' she said lightly, now understanding the reason for his reserve; he thought she would wake up this morning and regret the night they had spent together.

He sighed. 'Yes. God, I knew I shouldn't have let it happen.' He fell back against his pillow, his arms above his head as he stared up at the ceiling. 'But I was greedy,' he muttered. 'I couldn't say no when the opportunity was given to me. Fool,' he groaned. 'Fool, fool, *fool*!'

'Sin——'

'Did I forget something else?' he bit out grimly, angry at his own stupidity.

Robyn moved to lean on her elbow looking down at him. 'You forgot the fact that I haven't said any of those things, you have,' she teased gently, feeling an overwhelming tenderness towards the man whose body lay so warmly against her own.

He turned slowly to look at her, uncertainty in his eyes. 'Say something,' he invited gruffly.

'Thank you,' she breathed softly.

'Hm?' he was stunned into surprise.

Robyn smiled serenely, smoothing the frown from his brow. 'Last night was the most incredible night of my entire life,' she told him honestly.

'It was?'

She laughed at his incredulity. 'Can you doubt it?' she taunted her own uninhibited responses to him during the night.

Sin grimaced. 'When I'm with you like this I forget my own name!'

'Well last night you lived up to it! Now I have personal experience of the saying "wicked as sin". You are you know, very wicked,' but she didn't sound as if she minded that in the least.

'Am I?' he ran his thumbtip over her nipple as her breasts rested against his chest.

She trembled in reaction. 'You know you are. Don't do that!' she quivered, beginning to tremble as the now familiar warmth invaded her body, a fact he was well aware of as he moved to pin her beneath him.

It was over an hour later when they finally managed to leave Sin's bed and go down and prepare a late breakfast together. Robyn had to laugh when Sin proceeded to produce four or five assorted cartons of pre-cooked breakfast food.

'Do you always live like this?' she mocked as they helped themselves to the food straight from the foil trays once it had been heated.

'It saves on washing-up,' he nodded, having taken the time to shower and shave, the squareness of his jaw bare of stubble now, his hair still damp, his only clothing a short black towelling robe.

Robyn had opted for one of his shirts instead of the robe, feeling slightly ridiculous when she tried on the latter and the sleeves reached down to her knees. The black silk shirt Sin had worn the evening before lay against her skin like a caress, although that too reached down to her knees, the sleeves turned back to her elbows.

She grinned at him. 'I think I like living decadently for a change.'

Some of the laughter left his face, although it was quickly masked as he stood up. 'In that case, let's go back to bed!'

'Sin!' she squealed as he swung her up into his arms. 'Shouldn't a man of your mature years be taking things a little slower?' she mocked.

'Oh I'll be slow, Robyn.' There was a dangerous glitter in his eyes, a promise of things to come. 'I'll be very, very slow,' he told her with satisfaction.

And he was, exquisitely so, Robyn sobbing for his possession, a possession he relentlessly denied her as he took her again and again to peaks of ecstasy.

'Torturer!' she groaned, her head moving from side to side on the pillow as the mindless pleasure continued to torment her.

He raised his head to look at her with glowing blue eyes. 'I intend to imprint myself on your body so well you'll never be able to forget me,' he told her roughly, renewing his pleasure-giving caresses.

'I never could,' she gasped.

'I'm not taking any chances,' he said grimly, at last joining his body to hers, thrusting into her deeply, Robyn more than ready for him.

And if she had thought the night incredibly sensual the day was even more so, Sin finding new plateaus of desire for them to scale together, so that by the time she heard the ringing of her telephone at four o'clock that afternoon she felt as if she were merely an extension of the man himself, that they now shared something really special.

'Where are you going?' Sin asked dazedly as she dashed to the cottage door.

'Telephone,' she told him breathlessly, holding his shirt more securely about her.

'They'll call back——'

'It might be Brad,' she said agitatedly, hurrying into the adjoining cottage without a second glance.

It was Brad, ringing to tell her he would be bringing the children back now, that she could expect them in an hour or so. She didn't get to talk to Kim and Andy, but just the thought that they were coming home was enough to put a glow in her eyes and a happy curve to her mouth.

Sin had dressed and was in the kitchen drinking coffee at the kitchen table when she let herself in, and Robyn instantly sensed something different about him, although she didn't quite know what it was.

'It was Brad,' she told him quietly.

'Yes?' He continued to drink his coffee.

She frowned at his lack of warmth after the hours they had just spent together. 'He's going to drive the twins back now,' she explained.

'Good,' he nodded.

'Sin?' Her confusion deepened, hardly recognising him as the man who had made love to her continuously through the night and day. 'What's wrong?' she prompted.

'Wrong?' His eyes were hard as he looked at her, a cool icy blue. 'What could possibly be wrong?' he rasped.

'I don't know,' she shook her head, swallowing

hard. Was the weekend over, was that it? Had he reversed the roles on her and made her the one night stand he had accused her of trying to make him? Hadn't the hours she had spent in his arms meant the same to him?

The mug he had been drinking from landed on the table with a loud clatter, making Robyn jump nervously. 'You run out of here wearing only my shirt just so that you can talk to your ex-husband on the telephone, you come back to me after speaking to him with the sort of smile on your lips I'd walk through hot coals for and you *don't know what's wrong*!' he shouted fiercely.

Her heart had leapt at the admission about hot coals, having received no verbal declaration of love from him during their long night together, although she had been sure he couldn't have made love to her the way he had if he didn't feel something more for her than desire.

'What's wrong is that you aren't married to him any longer,' Sin bit out roughly.

'I know that, but I knew he would be calling me about bringing the twins——'

'I don't believe that's the reason you ran to talk to him,' he told her viciously, his eyes blazing.

'Sin, please listen to me——'

'No, *you* listen to me!' he ordered angrily. 'I'm not going to accept being made into someone you come to for a little physical comfort. I was wrong when I said you made the mistake last night, I'm the one that did that, thinking I could seriously mean anything to you——'

'But you do,' she protested.

'Do you love me?' he asked scornfully.

Colour deepened her cheeks. Love? Not once during their night and day together had she allowed herself to think of her feelings for this man, knowing that whatever it was she did feel for him it was still too young and vulnerable to be analysed into a category.

'No, of course you don't,' he dismissed disgustedly. 'And I don't suppose you want anything more to do with me now either!'

'It will be a little difficult when the twins get back——'

'Why?' he cut in ruthlessly.

'Well—Because——'

'Why should my spending all my evenings with you now be any different to the past week?'

The colour in her cheeks wouldn't seem to recede. 'I wasn't thinking of the evenings——'

'And I certainly wasn't talking about the nights,' he rasped harshly. 'Do you really imagine I would run the risk of the children seeing us together—like that?'

She looked at him appealingly. 'I don't understand what you want from me. Didn't you enjoy last night?' She was sure it had been as pleasurable for him as it had for her.

'You know I did,' he snapped. 'But I've never been subjected to the role of sexual plaything before, and I'm not about to start now.'

'Sexual plaything!' she spluttered disbelievingly. 'Sin, you have to be joking!'

'Do I?' he scorned bitterly. 'What else was last night about if it wasn't sex?'

'Don't make it seem as if last night was all my fault,' she was becoming angry herself now. 'You were there too, you know!'

'I know exactly where I was,' he met her gaze challengingly. 'But like I said, it was a mistake.'

'Well that's just fine!' she snapped, turning to go up the stairs. 'I'll get dressed and then leave.'

'Robyn——'

'Don't say any more, Sin,' she told him through tight lips, her control dangerously close to slipping. 'Not if you want to allow me to leave with any dignity at all.'

He seemed to be about to say something and then changed his mind, turning away to stare out of the kitchen window, his shoulders hunched over, his hands thrust into his pockets. She turned with a choked cry and ran up the stairs, made to feel even worse as she donned what was obviously a dress meant to be worn in the evening rather than late afternoon. The fact that she had nothing else here to wear, having discarded Sin's shirt on the rumpled unmade bed, made her feel cheap and nasty, making the time she had spent with Sin seem the same way.

What was the matter with him that he should be acting this way? He was reacting how *she* should have reacted, accusing her of using him, of having no deeper feelings for him than the sexual ones. If the whole situation weren't so depressingly painful it would be laughable!

He hadn't moved when she returned down the stairs, and the rigidity of his stiffly held back didn't encourage her to talk to him again, to try and make him understand. She closed the cottage door behind her, straightening her shoulders so he wouldn't see just how upset she was.

That pride lasted her until she closed her own cottage door behind her, and then a desolation more intense than the previous day washed over her, leaving her emotionally broken.

But none of that distress showed when Brad

arrived back with the children shortly after five, and after their initial greetings she faced Brad while the twins went to wash for tea.

His gaze was speculative on her pale face. 'You were a long time answering the telephone this afternoon.'

She shrugged. 'I was busy.'

'You sounded breathless.'

'Did I?' she dismissed. 'I don't remember.'

'I see Thornton is back,' Brad raised dark brows in mocking query.

'Yes.' She turned back to the work-top, arranging cakes on a plate, her hands shaking slightly.

'Still not friends?' Brad taunted, watching in amusement as one of the cakes fell out of her hand to the floor.

'Well, don't just stand there,' she snapped from her bending position as she picked up the biggest pieces of the broken cake. 'Get me a cloth.'

He didn't hurry himself as he did so, dropping the cloth into her impatiently waiting hand. 'Hit a raw nerve, did I?' he mocked as she accidentally threw the cloth into the bin along with the discarded cake, impatiently retrieving it to wash it under the running tap. 'Or did I hit several?' he mused.

'Mind your own business, Brad.'

'You're doing it again,' he mocked smilingly. 'Acting defensively is a sure sign that something's wrong.'

The cloth landed in the sink with a squelchy splash as she threw it down to turn on him angrily. 'I'm sick and tired of amateur psychiatrists analysing my actions this weekend,' she told him heatedly. 'Telling you to mind your own business isn't acting defensively, it's doing exactly what it sounds like.'

'Who else has been analysing you? Sin?' Brad wasn't at all put off by her anger. 'Have the two of you made up and argued again all in the space of one day?'

'Why don't you——'

'My God, you have,' he laughed. 'You never used to be this fiery, Robyn.'

'I'm well aware of the fact that I used to be your doormat——'

'You're getting nasty now.' The amusement had gone from his face and voice.

She had also done nothing but argue with him lately when usually she couldn't be bothered with such things.

'I'm sorry, Brad.' She put a hand up to her temple. 'This weekend hasn't been a good time for me. I've missed the twins dreadfully.'

'They've missed you too,' he told her dryly.

'They have?' she frowned.

'Did you think they wouldn't?' he scoffed her stupidity.

'They seemed to be having such a good time when I telephoned yesterday . . .' She shook her head. 'I thought they would be too busy to even think of me.'

'Maybe they were, until it came to bed time.' He grimaced. 'I didn't catch on to the glass of water routine at all. I was just damned angry when they kept calling out like that. I think I went down a couple of notches in their estimation.'

'I'm sure you didn't,' she could afford to be generous now that she knew the twins had missed her.

'Maybe not,' he shrugged dismissively. 'Anyway, I leave for South Africa in the week, I'll give you a call when I get back.'

It was his usual casual parting, and she knew it could be months before they saw him again. She was even secretly—and selfishly—a little pleased that she would have Kim and Andy exclusively to herself for several weeks.

But the two children who sat down to tea with her were nothing like the two that had left so excitedly for London the previous evening, and she felt guilty for her own elation in Brad's absence; the children were sure to feel the parting more after being with him for the weekend.

'Did you have a good time?' she tried to draw them into conversation as they merely picked at their food rather than eating it, an unusual occurrence when they both had such healthy appetites.

'Yes.' As usual it was Andy that answered for both of them, not looking up from his plate.

'How is your cold, Kim?' she tried another approach.

'Better,' her daughter answered flatly.

'So what did you and Daddy do over the weekend?' she asked brightly.

'We went shopping.' Once again it was Andy that answered her. 'And then last night Daddy took us out to a proper restaurant. Today we just spent at his flat.'

'Well you couldn't go out all the time.' She stood up to clear away, most of the food left untouched. 'Daddy has been working all week, I suppose he was tired.'

'Oh we didn't mind staying in,' her son shook

his head. 'He has a video and lots of films we could look at.'

'And what was Daddy doing while you looked at the video?' her question was made casually enough, although the twins' subdued behaviour disturbed her a little; they had become used to only seeing Brad occasionally over the years.

'He was—Ouch!' Kim grimaced, glaring at Andy, who looked suspiciously innocent all of a sudden. 'He was busy,' she finished awkwardly.

'What——'

'Would you mind if we went to bed now, Mummy?' Andy cut in firmly.

'Bed?' she repeated frowningly. 'But it's only a quarter past six.' And at least an hour earlier than the usual time she had to persuade them to go to bed.

'We're tired,' Andy insisted stubbornly.

'Well if that's what you both want . . .' She shrugged resignedly.

Although nothing was said as she bathed them and put them to bed Robyn couldn't help the concern she felt. It couldn't just be the prospect of Brad's absence for a few weeks that was making the children behave like this, something must have gone gravely wrong this weekend for them to be so subdued. Her own worry about this unusual occurrence of a weekend with their father returned with a vengeance, and she wished she had someone she could talk to about that worry; she wished she and Sin were still friends!

CHAPTER EIGHT

The cry and then the loud sobbing woke her instantly, and she hastily scrambled out of bed to run to the twins' bedroom. Kim sat up in the bed crying brokenly, Andy beside her as he tried to comfort her.

'Be quiet,' he hissed. 'You'll wake Mummy.'

'But I want her!' Kim howled, crying louder than ever.

'You'll only worry her,' Andy told her forcefully. 'Now be quiet, you little——'

'I'm already here, Andy,' she interrupted him slowly. 'And I'm already worried.' She took Kim in her arms, tightening her hold as her daughter buried her face against her neck. The brief conversation she had overheard as she came into the room gave her a feeling of unease; never before had either of her children shied away from telling her if they were troubled or upset about something. 'What's wrong, darling?' she smoothed Kim's silky hair.

'I——'

'She just had a bad dream, Mummy,' Andy interrupted his sister with a fierce look at Kim.

'Andy!' Robyn quietly reprimanded before looking down at Kim's tear-stained face. 'Is that what happened, baby, did you have a bad dream?'

Kim glanced at her brother before answering. 'Yes,' she nodded.

Robyn wasn't at all fooled by that answer, and she was determined to get to the bottom of their

strange behaviour since they got home, was sure
Kim's crying had something to do with that. 'Is
that the truth?' she prompted softly. 'Or did
something happen while you were away this
weekend to upset you?'

Once again Kim looked at her twin for
guidance. 'It was just a bad dream, Mummy,' she
muttered.

She frowned, knowing she was being lied to.
And it wasn't something either of her children
usually did, making her worry all the more.

'Has Sin gone away?'

She was taken aback by the unexpectedness of
the question. 'No . . .' she answered Kim dazedly.

'I want to see him.'

'He's asleep, darling,' she chided softly. 'It's
one o'clock in the morning.'

Kim's bottom lip trembled precariously before
she began to cry once again. 'He's gone away,'
she sobbed. 'I know he has.'

'His car is parked outside, Kim——'

'Then why didn't he come to see us when we
got home?' she sniffed.

Robyn felt guilty as she realised she was
probably to blame for that; after the way she and
Sin had parted earlier he probably thought he
wasn't welcome here, not even to see the twins.
'He's been busy, darling——'

'Not that busy,' Kim pouted mutinously.

'Darling——'

'I want to see him,' her daughter repeated with
a choked sob.

She chewed worriedly on her bottom lip as she
recognised all the classic signs of Kim bringing
on one of her now rare asthmatic attacks. They
had terrified Robyn when Kim was younger, but

they seemed to be happening less as she got older, although when they did occur they were stronger and more frightening, hence her worry over Kim's slight cold the previous day.

'I'll go and see if he's still up,' she told Kim. 'But if he isn't you'll have to wait until tomorrow to see him,' she warned sternly, her daughter receiving no concessions on her behaviour just because she had these attacks; that wouldn't have been fair on Andy.

She didn't particularly relish the thought of going over to get Sin, but as she pulled on a robe over her nightgown to ward off the chill of the evening she could see a light on in his lounge; maybe he had finally decided to start work on his book. And she didn't think he would mind her interrupting him when he knew it was for Kim, having a genuine affection for both children.

She felt ridiculously conspicuous as she waited for him to answer her knock on the door, although they had no near neighbours to talk of, the nearest houses already in darkness.

Sin looked harassed when he opened the door to her, his trousers and shirt rumpled, the latter unbuttoned down his chest, his hair looking as if he had run his hands through it several times in either frustration or anger. His eyes narrowed as he looked at her. 'Yes?'

His tone wasn't very encouraging, but the memory of Kim's swollen and blotchy face urged her on. 'I know it's late——'

'It is,' he agreed coldly. 'Very late.'

Her eyes widened at the aggression in his voice. 'Yes. Well I came over to——'

'Aren't you a little nervous about leaving Kim and Andy on their own?' he cut in icily.

She frowned at his censorious tone. 'I'll only be a minute, and they——'

'Surely longer than a minute, Robyn,' he taunted challengingly. 'I may find you irresistible, but I think that tonight I may need more than a little encouragement.'

'Encouragement?' she repeated dazedly. 'What are you talking about?' she demanded impatiently, moving awkwardly from one slippered foot to the other.

'Don't deny that you came over here with the intention of going to bed with me——'

'You arrogant bastard!' A white-hot tide of anger washed over her, her hand coming up to strike him forcefully across the cheek. 'Do you seriously think I crept over here in the dead of night for a quick romp in bed while my children are asleep?' she asked contemptuously.

His hand had moved instinctively to his cheek, flexing his jaw slightly. 'Obviously not,' he drawled in a pained voice.

'Of course not! I came because Kim woke up in hysterics and asked for you,' she bit out furiously. 'But it's obvious you can't get your mind—or anything else—out of the bedroom!' She turned away disgustedly, only to be stopped from walking away by Sin's powerful grip on her arm. 'Let go of me,' she ordered between gritted teeth, her head thrown back as she looked at him, no remorse in her face for the livid fingermarks he had now revealed on his rigidly taut cheek.

'Is Kim ill?' he wanted to know, all mockery gone from his voice now.

'You aren't really interested——'

'Is she ill, damn you!' His fingers dug painfully into her flesh.

Robyn shook her head. 'She had a bad dream——'

'And she asked for me?'

'Yes.' Her head went back in challenge; it wasn't easy admitting that one of her children had asked for someone other than her when they were upset, especially as this man had been a complete stranger to them all until a week ago.

Sin released her abruptly. 'I'll come with you,' he moved out of the cottage.

'If you're sure you can spare the time,' she nodded stiffly.

His mouth tightened. 'Look, I know I was rough on you a few minutes ago, but——'

'I don't care to discuss your mistaken assumption, Mr Thornton,' she told him coldly. 'But needless to say I would never have come to your cottage tonight if Kim wasn't so upset.'

'Robyn——'

She ignored the pleading in his face and voice, pushing open the door to the twins' bedroom, her heart contracting painfully as both children launched themselves into his arms as she stood in the doorway feeling superfluous.

Sin looked at her over the top of identical red heads, holding a child in each arm, his expression compassionate as he saw the pain in her eyes. 'How about some hot milk?' he suggested to her gruffly.

'They don't——'

'Hot milk sounds lovely,' Andy instantly agreed.

Robyn blinked at him blankly; neither Andy or Kim had ever liked hot milk.

'Robyn?' Sin prompted hardly.

'I—Yes,' she agreed dazedly, halfway down the

stairs before she realised what she had done. She was sure that they were *all* aware of the fact that the twins didn't like hot milk, and yet here she was meekly on her way downstairs to prepare two glasses! What made it worse was that both she and Sin knew the request had only been made to get her out of the room.

To keep herself busy, if not her mind active, she actually prepared the milk, although she knew it wasn't going to be needed, delaying her return upstairs as she could hear the steady murmur of Sin's voice. Although she was a little surprised when he came down alone a few minutes later.

'They're both asleep,' he explained at her questioning look as he entered the kitchen.

Her puzzled frown turned to one of disbelief. 'But a few minutes ago they were both almost in tears.'

He shrugged. 'I told you I have the sort of voice that can talk children to sleep.'

'Yes, but——' She shook her head. 'It seems incredible.'

'Go and see for yourself,' he invited. 'I turned off the main light and just left on the night-light, I hope that was all right.'

'Fine,' she answered in a preoccupied voice.

'We might as well drink the hot milk now,' he suggested softly.

Robyn looked up at him sharply. 'I'm sure you must have some work to get back to,' her voice was hard as she once again recalled his reaction to her interruption a few minutes ago, the slap she had given him having faded to a dull red now.

His mouth tightened at the dismissal. 'Nothing that can't wait. And we have to talk——'

'I don't think so,' she shook her head.

'About Kim,' he finished pointedly. 'I take it you do want to know what has disturbed her?'

She flushed at the rebuke. 'Of course I do,' she snapped.

'Then I suggest we sit down in comfort and drink the milk while we talk about it.'

'She told you?'

'Yes.'

'All right,' she agreed ungraciously, puzzled at her children being able to talk to this man and not her; hurt too. 'But I will just go up and check on them first.' She didn't wait for his reaction to this, verbal or otherwise, going up the stairs without sparing him a glance.

As he had already told her, Kim and Andy were fast asleep, an untroubled sleep by the look of their angelic faces above the neatly tucked in bedclothes, Kim not even having bothered with the doll she usually cuddled up to, Robyn picking it up from where it lay unwanted on the floor, holding it to her protectively as she realised she had Sin to thank for their apparent calm after the storm.

'And they're both still breathing too.'

She turned sharply at the sound of that softly mocking voice, Sin standing in the open doorway, his expression taunting.

'Just in case you think I'm a mass murderer of children,' he drawled.

She gave him a scathing look as she brushed past him out of the room. 'Don't be ridiculous,' she snapped irritably once they were far enough away not to disturb the children.

Sin stood across the lounge from her. 'Was I being? A few minutes ago I had the distinct impression that you hated the sight of me.'

'I don't hate you, but I hate what you're trying to do to me.'

'And what's that?' His eyes were narrowed.

'Make me feel guilty about a night that was mutually enjoyed, making it seem cheap and nasty.'

'Robyn——'

'Could we please just talk about Kim,' she dismissed agitatedly, sitting down to broodingly sip at the warmly comforting milk, not having the same aversion to it that Kim and Andy did. 'You said you know what's disturbing her?' she prompted worriedly.

Sin nodded, sitting opposite her, also sipping the milk. 'Did you know that Brad introduced them both to his current girlfriend while they were staying with him this weekend? I can see that you didn't,' he frowned as she blanched.

'No,' she acknowledged faintly.

'Well he did,' Sin sighed. 'It seems they all went out to dinner together last night, and that Tina, that's the woman's name, spent the day with them today, too.'

Why would Brad do such a thing, unless he were actually serious about the woman! The repercussions that could occur from that made her pale even more. The only possible reason Brad *could* have for introducing his children to this woman were if he were serious about her, in fact hadn't he made a veiled reference about entering the state of 'domestic bliss' again before he left yesterday? Could that really be a possibility? And if it were, why had he taken the twins to London to meet the other woman, he certainly didn't need their approval.

'You didn't know anything about this?' Sin frowned at her continued silence.

'No,' she shook her head.

'Brad hadn't told you about this woman?'

'Oh, he may have made a few oblique references to the woman in his life,' she shrugged, her thoughts still racing. 'But he's never implied—never given the impression——'

'That this time he might be serious,' Sin finished grimly. 'Well apparently he is.'

Her gaze was sharp. 'How do you know that?'

'Tina asked the children how they would like living with their father in London all the time if the opportunity arose,' he revealed flatly.

Robyn paled to a sickly white. 'Brad couldn't do that . . .'

'Couldn't he?'

She shook her head in stunned denial of the idea. 'When we divorced he agreed I could have the children.'

'It looks as if he may have changed his mind,' Sin told her grimly.

'No,' she said shakily. 'I don't believe it. I've never stopped him seeing the children any time he wanted to.'

'Maybe it's no longer enough for him.'

'But he doesn't even *like* children.'

'Not even his own?'

'Not for too long, no,' she admitted awkwardly.

Sin shrugged. 'Love does strange things to people. How would it look to this woman if he said he didn't want his own children?'

Her face was haunted. 'You think that's what may have happened?'

'I think it's a possibility,' he sighed. 'And so do the twins. They don't want to go and live with their father.'

'But they love Brad!'

'Not as much as they love you—and certainly not enough to go and live with him.'

'They told you that?' she frowned.

'Yes.'

'But why didn't they tell me what was worrying them?' she cried out her pain. 'I could have told them it would never happen.'

'I'm not so sure you could have, not with any degree of certainty,' Sin said slowly. 'And they told me because they seem to think I can do something to stop it.'

'What?'

'I think I'm supposed to come up with a solution all on my own,' he drawled.

'I had no idea it would be anything like this,' she murmured softly. 'And what do you mean, I couldn't be certain?' she demanded. 'There's no way Brad can take Kim and Andy away from me without my consent, and I'll never give it.'

'Robyn,' Sin's voice was gentle. 'If Brad can prove you're an unfit mother——'

'How dare you even suggest such a thing!' she flared, standing up indignantly, unaware of how young and beautiful she looked in the chocolate brown robe and pale green nightgown. 'I've dedicated my entire life to them, I——'

'I know,' he interrupted softly. 'But try looking at this from an outsider's point of view. You live in a cottage courtesy of Brad's uncle——'

'I pay rent!'

'I'm sure you do,' he nodded. 'But I doubt it's that much, certainly lower than if you were renting off anyone else.' Her blush gave truth to that. 'And you also work for Brad's uncle, hours that you fit in with your own schedule with the twins. Without those concessions I doubt you would be able to manage the way you do.'

'The Colonel would never ask us to leave,' she said with certainty.

'I'm sure he wouldn't. I've learnt this last week that he's a very straightforward and honest man. But if Brad should try to make a case against you based on the fact that you still rely very heavily on him and his family for your support then you could find yourself in difficulties. I'm not saying you would,' he added hastily. 'Only that maybe, just maybe, you could.'

Robyn became very still as something else occurred to her. 'Brad has been very interested in whether or not I have a man in my life,' she revealed stiltedly, slowly becoming convinced that Sin was right; Brad did intend trying to take the children from her. 'He—He asked a lot of questions about you,' she swallowed hard. 'I told him he was imagining things when he accused me of being involved with you, but—Oh God, this is awful!' She buried her face in her hands.

'It's all right, Robyn,' Sin took her in his arms, resting her face against his chest. 'There's nothing about our relationship that he can use against you.'

'There's last night,' she choked.

'The twins weren't at home then.'

'But they are now. No one would believe you came over here solely to see Kim if they knew we were together last night too.'

'I didn't.'

'Didn't what?' she looked up at him with tear-wet eyes.

Sin's expression softened as she looked down at her. 'Didn't come over here solely for Kim's benefit. I could see that *you* needed me. Do you know how good it feels to know you needed me, for whatever reason?'

'Sin——'

'I know my timing is lousy,' he groaned, his eyes darkening. 'But I have to kiss you.'

Her lips parted invitingly beneath his, her head bent backwards under the pressure of his kiss, the caress all the more intense because of their already heightened emotions.

'God, I've missed you since you walked out on me this afternoon,' he rested his forehead on hers, the pressure of his arms about her moulding her body to his.

'You wanted me to go,' she reminded him.

'What I really wanted was—Now isn't the time to discuss that,' he sighed as he probed the shadows in her eyes. 'You look tired out,' he said concernedly. 'If you get a good night's sleep—what's left of it—things might not seem so bad in the morning.'

'I think they might seem worse,' she groaned. 'I can't believe anyone would be cruel enough to let Brad take my children away from me.'

'They probably won't,' he assured her gently. 'But things could get pretty nasty if Brad should try.'

'I can't see him doing that to Kim and Andy.' But her voice lacked conviction as she silently acknowledged that Brad was capable of anything to get something he wanted. And if he were serious enough about this woman Tina . . .!

'Let's hope not.' But Sin didn't seem convinced of the fact either. 'Now I'm going to put you to bed—*put* you to bed, Robyn,' he bit out tautly at her dismayed expression. 'Not share it with you!'

'I'm sorry,' she was instantly contrite for her suspicions. 'I'm just so upset about all this I don't know what I'm doing.'

His face softened. 'That's why I'm putting you to bed.' He turned with his arm still about her shoulders and led the way up to her bedroom, taking off her robe for her as if she were a child, before tucking her comfortably beneath the covers, much as he must have done with the twins earlier. 'Now,' he sat down on the side of her bed. 'You are not to think about this any more tonight—I know that's easier said than done,' he said ruefully at her sceptical expression, 'but if you're exhausted tomorrow it isn't going to help matters. Kim and Andy need your assurances that nothing is going to change in their lives, and if you walk around looking like a zombie with a permanent worried look on your face they are just going to feel more insecure than they do now.'

She knew he was right, but she just wasn't tired, had too much on her mind to be able to sleep.

'Close your eyes,' he instructed. 'And listen to me.'

Like an obedient child she did as he told her, trying to concentrate as he began to talk about the book he intended writing based on some of the Colonel's war experiences.

The next thing Robyn knew the alarm on her bedside table was going off, and she turned to switch it off, her eyes widening as she saw the man who slept in her bedroom chair, his long length coiled uncomfortably into its dainty smallness. The alarm hadn't woken him, and for a few brief moments she allowed herself the indulgence of imagining she could wake up in the same room as him every morning. It was a heady thought.

But it was an impossible one; after what the twins had revealed last night about their father she didn't even know if she dare see Sin again, knew Brad was capable of using the friendship against her if he had to.

Which reminded her, Sin shouldn't be here with her now! She got quietly out of bed, shaking Sin gently by the shoulder, gratified when he woke without making a sound. 'Come down to the kitchen and have some coffee,' she urged in a whisper.

He blinked dazedly as he took stock of his surroundings, running a hand around the back of his neck as he stretched his stiffened muscles. 'God, did I really fall asleep here?' he groaned as he uncoiled his lean length from the chair, his discomfort obvious.

'Yes,' she confirmed quietly. 'Now would you come downstairs before the twins come in here and find you.'

'I forgot,' he grimaced, following her to the door, catching sight of his own reflection in the mirror as he passed her dressing-table. 'God, what a mess I am,' he muttered as they went down the stairs.

Robyn couldn't altogether agree with him, found his sleep-mussed appearance highly disturbing, his hair lightly tousled, his eyes warm, lacking the angry coldness she had seen all too often lately, exuding a male attraction that he was completely unaware of.

'Look at it this way,' she teased as she prepared the coffee, relieved at having got down to the kitchen without being detected by Kim and Andy, 'at least you haven't got to go home in an evening dress!'

He grimaced as he sprawled on a kitchen stool. 'I didn't mean to fall asleep in your bedroom.'

'It seems you can talk yourself to sleep as well as everyone else!'

'I've never talked a woman to sleep before, especially when we've been in bed,' he added wickedly.

'Sin!'

'It certainly is,' he grinned as she blushed. 'A waste too. You seem in a better mood this morning?' he looked at her questioningly.

She avoided his gaze. 'As you said, things often seem better in the light of day.'

'They do?' he sipped his coffee with obvious relish.

'Yes,' she insisted firmly.

'How much better?'

She shrugged. 'I'm going to telephone Brad today, see if we can't sort things out.'

'Do you think that's a good idea,' Sin frowned. 'Surely if he had wanted to discuss his plans with you he would have done so by now?'

'What other choice do I have?' she snapped irritably, not exactly welcoming the idea of calling Brad, without Sin putting the dampener on it. 'I can't let things just linger on, not when Kim and Andy are being affected.'

'I'm not sure confronting him with it is the right thing to do——'

'Did I ask for your opinion?' she flared. 'I'm grateful for the way you helped out last night, but——'

'Are you?' he put down his empty cup. 'I

doubt it,' he rasped. 'But I have a responsibility to Kim and Andy. They're expecting me to perform some sort of miracle and make their world right again.'

'They're old enough to know that life doesn't work out that way——'

'At least give me a chance,' he ground out.

'To do what?'

'I'm going up to London today, I could make discreet enquiries about Brad and his girlfriend.'

'What would be the point of that?' she frowned.

'At least then you would know what you're dealing with, and without antagonising Brad,' he explained impatiently. 'Why risk making an issue out of something the twins may just have misunderstood?'

His reasoning sounded logical, and yet she was loath to be beholden to this man for anything else.

'I'm going to London, anyway,' he encouraged, at her hesitation, guessing the reason for it. 'Waiting one day isn't going to make much difference to your own plans.'

'No,' she acknowledged softly. 'All right, Sin,' she nodded decisively. 'But you will be discreet?'

'Aren't I sitting in your kitchen right now as if I've just arrived?' he taunted. 'That was the idea behind rushing me down here, wasn't it?'

'Yes,' she blushed. 'I nearly died when I woke up and found you asleep in my room.'

'It was certainly a novel way of spending the night together!'

The sarcastic rejoiner she had been going to make was halted by the boisterous arrival of Kim and Andy, both children excited by the fact that Sin had come over to have breakfast with them!

It was a very long day for Robyn as she waited to hear from Sin, although at least she didn't have to put up with Caroline's bitchiness, the other woman having decided to stay on in London for another day. If it weren't for her worry over Brad possibly remarrying it would have been a quietly pleasant day for her.

The telephone was ringing as she let herself into the cottage, and she picked up the receiver, reciting her number breathlessly, having been aware of its ringing all the time she was trying to unlock the door.

'Robyn?' barked a disgruntled voice.

'Brad!' she realised uncertainly, surprised to hear from him when yesterday he had given the impression he wouldn't be contacting them for some weeks.

'What the hell do you mean by letting me hear of your engagement from a third person?' he exploded. 'And that third person in particular!'

'W . . . what?' she breathed dazedly, this the last thing she had expected to hear.

'I have just been talking to your fiancé, and believe me I am not amused,' Brad ground out.

She could tell that, and neither was she! What was he talking about? 'What fiancé?' she asked in a bewildered voice.

'Sin Thornton,' he bit out grimly. 'He's just told me the two of you are getting married!'

CHAPTER NINE

'MARRIED?' she repeated dumbfoundedly. 'Did you say *married*?'

'Don't try and bluff your way out of this, Robyn,' he told her coldly. 'I heard it from the man himself.'

She was well aware of that, knew that he couldn't have heard it anywhere else and have actually believed it. She just couldn't imagine what had prompted Sin to make such a claim. And rather than trying to 'bluff her way *out* of this' situation, she was going to have difficulty keeping up with the pretence, having no idea why Sin had told Brad. 'Er—What exactly did he tell you?' she delayed.

'He wouldn't have told me anything at all if I hadn't happened to run into him just as I was leaving a restaurant,' Brad said aggressively. 'Just when was I going to hear of this marriage from you—when it was already a fact?'

She couldn't help wondering how deliberate that 'running into' Sin had been! But she also didn't like Brad's attitude when he talked of her remarrying. 'Don't worry, Brad, I would have sent you an invitation!'

'From what Thornton said I doubt I'll be in the country!' he rasped.

'And what did Sin say?' her voice was still sharp with sarcasm.

'Just that you're getting married, and soon. But I don't need to tell you that,' he dismissed angrily. 'You're well aware of your own plans.'

She only wished she were! This surely couldn't be Sin's idea of discretion!

'Don't you think you're being a little hasty marrying a man you've only known for a week?' he scorned.

'It's ten days, actually,' she derided tautly, getting angrier and angrier at his assumption that he had the right to censure her actions.

'Don't be so damned petty, Robyn,' he bit out angrily. 'You hardly know the man.'

'Better than you think,' she drawled.

'Going to bed with a man isn't knowing him!'

She was glad he couldn't see the livid colour in her cheeks. 'I know that,' she snapped. 'I wasn't talking about sex, Brad. Sin is a kind, protective, very gentle man.'

'He's also a ruthless reporter,' Brad reminded tauntingly. 'That is what you once called me, isn't it?'

He knew it was, damn him. 'Sin is no longer in that profession,' she bit out.

'"Once a reporter always a reporter",' once again he gave her back one of her own quotations.

'Not Sin,' she staunchly defended.

There was silence for several minutes. 'So you really are going to marry him,' Brad said slowly.

'I—Probably,' she evaded.

'When?'

'I—er—We haven't set an exact date yet.'

'Thornton sounded as if he were impatient for the day,' Brad derided mockingly.

'Shouldn't he be?' she returned defensively. 'You once were,' she reminded hardly.

'So I was,' he derided, his anger seeming to have faded to sarcasm now.

'Which reminds me,' she said slowly, finding

the perfect opening to introduce the subject of his own possible marriage. 'Kim and Andy mentioned meeting a friend of yours called Tina this weekend,' her voice was deliberately casual.

'Yes?' Brad was now as defensive as she had been minutes earlier.

'They just mentioned meeting her,' she dismissed lightly.

'Is there anything wrong in my introducing them to one of my friends?'

'Nothing at all. I just wondered if—er—if she's a good friend?'

'About as good as Thornton is to you,' he answered resentfully.

'Does that mean you're also thinking of getting married?' She held her breath as she waited for his answer.

'I may be,' he hedged. 'It depends.'

Robyn tensed. 'On what?'

'On a number of things,' he returned agitatedly.

'Such as?' she persisted, despite knowing she was antagonising him. She needed to *know*, and he was her only source. Only he could tell her what his future plans were, although he seemed reluctant to do so, making her all the more wary.

'Such as things that don't concern you,' he told her concisely. 'When and if they do I'll let you know.'

She bit back her angry retort with effort, knowing it would do no good to make him so angry he put the telephone down on her; she would learn nothing that way.

'And in the meantime I'm not sure I approve of your marrying Thornton——'

'I wasn't aware that I had asked for your approval——'

'You'll need it if he's going to be a father to my children!' Brad bit out angrily.

Robyn bristled resentfully. 'Nowhere in our divorce settlement does it say you have to approve of any subsequent marriage I may make,' she told him tautly.

'All right, let me put it this way,' he said with ill-concealed impatience. 'Don't you think you're being a little impetuous by marrying a man you've only known a week—ten days?' he amended dryly.

'When you fall in love you don't estimate how long it took, you just know it happened.'

'And you're in love?' Brad scorned.

She moistened dry lips, the most predominant feeling she had towards Sin at the moment pure anger. None of this conversation need be taking place if he hadn't told Brad that ridiculous lie, at least, Brad wouldn't have been so resentful when she questioned him about Tina.

'I doubt if you know what love is.' Brad didn't even wait for her answer.

'Why you——'

'You didn't last time,' he pointed out with satisfaction.

'I soon learnt what love *wasn't*,' she returned heatedly, just about at the end of her patience with him.

'Me,' he acknowledged abruptly. 'But you think Sin Thornton is "it"?'

'*Yes!*'

'And nothing I can say will make you change your mind about marrying him?'

'Not a thing!'

Brad sighed. 'I suppose you're old enough to make your own mistakes.'

'More than old enough I would have said!' If he were actually here she knew she would have had trouble restraining herself from hitting him.

'Mm,' he still sounded as if he doubted it. 'We'll just have to wait and see, won't we?'

Robyn hated his patronising tone, knew it was unwarranted, that *he* had been the one to end their marriage, even if she had known it was all over between them. But for the moment she had no comeback, her anger fading to be replaced by a stark realisation, a realisation that terrified the life out of her.

'I have to go now, Brad,' she told him stiltedly. 'Kim and Andy will be home for their tea soon.'

'All right,' he grudgingly agreed. 'But I would appreciate it if any further information about your marriage came directly from you.'

She consented woodenly, ringing off to stare dazedly into space, too shocked to move.

She loved Sinclair Thornton!

She had realised it even as she hotly defended her feelings for him to Brad, had suddenly known it was the truth; she really did love Sin, whether she had known him a week, ten days, or ten *years*! She had tried to excuse the weekend she had spent with him as nothing more than a physical attraction after so many years of denial, but she had known other men during those years, men who wouldn't have been averse to making love to her with no strings attached, and she hadn't been interested in them. She should have realised her feelings towards Sin were different.

But how did he feel about her? He had told Brad they were getting married, but she felt sure that could only have been in retaliation to something Brad had said to him, that he didn't really mean it but had been antagonised into saying it. No doubt he would extricate himself from the situation as soon as he possibly could without making things too awkward. If only she knew what had prompted him to say it in the first place! Brad must have been particularly insulting.

It was a certainty Sin would never marry her. He was fond of the twins, physically attracted to her, but marriage . . .! He had managed to stay a bachelor for the last thirty-seven years, she doubted he would seriously consider changing that for a divorcee with two children.

Why was she even imagining it could come true, she was as unmarriageable as Caroline had once said she was when it came to a man like Sin!

She sighed as she stood up, going in to the kitchen to get Kim and Andy's tea, feeling a slight resentment towards them for the first time since they had been born. If she hadn't had them——

If she didn't have them she wouldn't have any life at all, they *were* her life! What she was suffering from was the age-old problem of a mother's love divided between her children and the man she loved. It was something she had never had to face before, and she daren't face it now, not when there was no real choice. She loved Kim and Andy more than her own life, and now she knew she loved Sin in the same way.

The children seemed to sense nothing different about her when they came bounding in for their tea, and why should they, she wasn't different; she had been in love with Sin for the last week, she just hadn't recognised it as love until now.

Kim and Andy were back to normal as they tucked into their tea, having childish confidence in Sin to make their world right again. And maybe they were right to do so; she had given Brad the perfect opportunity to tell her if he was going to marry Tina, and he hadn't taken it.

She was as tense as a coiled spring when she at last heard the Porsche turn into the neighbouring driveway. The twins were already in bed, both fast asleep after their restless sleep the night before, their trust secure in Sin's hands as far as they were concerned.

Robyn smoothed her hands over the cool brown sundress she wore, its thin shoulder-straps leaving a vast amount of her throat and arms bare, fitting over her breasts, a wide belt at her narrow waist. Her make-up was light and attractive, her hair secured loosely on top of her head in a tumble of curls, nothing at all like the secure bun she wore to go to work. Her appearance in the mirror showed a coolly serene young woman, but that appearance was deceptive; she was a bundle of nerves, suddenly shy at the thought of seeing Sin again.

He was bending down getting some things out of the back of his car when she reached his side, throwing his jacket over his arm as he straightened to look at her, lines of tiredness about his eyes.

'I have dinner ready,' she told him softly, concerned at how weary he looked.

He frowned. 'You couldn't have known when I would get back.'

'It's only a casserole,' she shrugged.

'I see,' he murmured, a little guarded with her, as if he weren't quite sure of her mood. 'Can I wash and change first? London leaves me feeling hot and sticky lately.'

'Take your time, the casserole won't spoil,' she nodded.

'I'll be over later, then.'

Robyn felt as if she had been dismissed. Oh, she knew she had been a little presumptuous in cooking dinner for him, but just because she had discovered she was in love with him didn't mean she should act any differently than she would have done if she hadn't realised her feelings for him. And in the circumstances, his making enquiries in London about Brad, it would have been only natural for her to prepare him dinner; goodness, she had been doing it all week, why stop now!

She had been fidgeting nervously in the kitchen for almost half an hour when he knocked on the door, tidying things that didn't need to be tidied, arranging and rearranging the flowers she had picked to go on the centre of the table.

Sin had changed into a very pale blue shirt and fitted denims, his hair still damp from the shower he had taken. He looked much less tired than he had a few minutes ago, although there was still a weary look to his eyes as she served the meal and sat opposite him.

'How are Kim and Andy today?' he asked after several minutes of silently eating.

Her mouth quirked without humour. 'Confident you can slay all their dragons.'

'But you don't think I can?' his eyes were narrowed.

She looked at him in challenge. 'I think,' she said slowly, 'that it depends how you go about it.'

Sin was suddenly still. 'You've heard from Brad, haven't you?' he realised flatly.

'Yes.' Her voice was deliberately even, giving away none of her emotions.

'What did he tell you?'

'Nothing at all about taking the twins from me.'

Sin sighed. 'Robyn——'

'What did *you* say to *him*?' she asked softly.

'He's already told you,' Sin breathed deeply. 'Hasn't he?'

'Yes.'

'And now you want to know what I thought I was doing saying something like that,' he grimaced.

'If you wouldn't mind,' she nodded calmly.

'I made the enquiries I said I would. And I did make them discreetly,' he stated firmly at her sceptical look. 'It was what I found out that made me search out Brad and act *in*discreetly.'

She frowned at this. 'What did you find out?'

'Tina is really Christina Fowler, her father owns the newspaper Brad works for.'

It was worse than anything she had imagined. If Tina's father owned a newspaper then it was obvious they were a rich family, and if she were she would have the means at her disposal to enter into a lengthy battle for the children.

'It's strongly rumoured that the two of them will be getting married soon,' Sin added at her prolonged silence.

She swallowed hard, pushing her plate away with the food almost untouched. 'When?'

He shrugged. 'Just soon, there hasn't been a date decided on yet. But I thought I would get in about the two of us before that happened.'

She looked at him with dull eyes. 'That we're getting married?'

'Yes.'

'When it isn't true?'

His mouth tightened. 'It was either that or he take the twins from you,' he bit out grimly.

'And what do you suppose will happen when the wedding doesn't take place?'

'It will.'

'I beg your pardon?' she gasped.

'We will be getting married, Robyn,' he looked at her with steady blue eyes.

'You—I—I can't let you do that, Sin,' she shook her head, tears glistening in her eyes.

His eyes were narrowed now. 'Do what?'

'Marry me for Kim and Andy's sake. I know how much you care for them, but I couldn't let any man marry me for that reason.' And she had thought she was unmarriageable *because* she had the twins!

Sin's mouth was a thin straight line. 'Then think of it as marrying me because we're good in bed together,' he rasped. 'Although with your limited experience you probably don't even realise that we are!'

He was being deliberately hurtful now, was taking pleasure in whiplashing her with his tongue—and she had no idea why. She was giving him a way out of an impulsive gesture, why didn't he just take it gracefully and leave?

'I realise, Sin,' she told him huskily.

'Do you?' he bit out harshly. 'Maybe I should just refresh your memory!'

'No——' her cry went unheeded as he stood up to pull her roughly into his arms, brutalising her mouth with a ruthlessness that brooked no denial. Robyn felt as if his tongue raped her as it marauded into her mouth, her slender frame crushed against him. 'Sin, no!' she finally managed to pull away from him enough to look up at him with pained eyes. 'This isn't the way, Sin,' she choked. 'If we married we would only end up hating each other.'

He looked down at her for a moment with glazed eyes, almost as if he was just realising what he had done. He thrust her away from him as if she burnt him, pushing his hands into his pockets. 'You would rather risk losing Kim and Andy than marry me?' he rasped harshly.

No, she would rather risk losing her beloved children than having Sin come to hate her! She nodded woodenly, not altogether surprised when he turned on his heel and left, the door closing forcefully behind him.

She was hollow-eyed and pale the next morning, hardly in the right frame of mind to spar with Caroline, the other woman having arrived back from London the evening before.

'I'm sure you all managed without me,' was the nearest she came to apologising for the way she had just gone off and left them to cope.

'Yes,' Robyn was too numb this morning to even be polite, having spent yet another almost sleepless night.

Caroline gave a disdainful sniff. 'Although if I had known Sin had gone I wouldn't have bothered to come back quite this soon.'

'Gone?' her voice was sharp. 'Sin's gone?'

The younger woman nodded. 'He left early this morning. Apparently he has all the information he needs and he's gone back to London.' The blue eyes filled with malice. 'Don't tell me he didn't let you know he was going?'

She shook her head, her spirits down to rock-bottom. She had taken the absence of the Porsche to simply mean Sin had gone out, she hadn't given a thought to the fact that he may have left altogether. She had intended going over to see him when he got back, had wanted them to be friends again at least.

'How naughty of him,' Caroline said with relish. 'And after the two of you—spent so much time together too,' she added with pointed accusation.

'He has come over several times to see the twins,' Robyn told her dully.

Caroline gave her a pitying glance. 'If you think anyone is going to believe that excuse you can forget it!'

She blushed. 'It's the truth.'

'Maybe it is,' Caroline conceded haughtily. 'But he certainly can't be visiting them at ten o'clock at night. The neighbours have been talking, Robyn,' she added at her questioning look. 'You've made an absolute fool of yourself over him, and the whole village knows it.'

'Caroline——'

'Oh don't worry, I'm not going to come out with a lot of recriminations——'

She glared at the younger girl. 'You don't know how happy that makes me!'

'There's no need to get annoyed,' Caroline disdained. 'Although I can understand your being a little upset; you obviously had no idea he was going to walk out on you.'

She held herself stiffly as she stood up. 'Sin did not walk out on me,' she said in a controlled voice. 'There was no relationship to walk out on. He was a guest of your uncle's, and now he's gone.'

'If that's what you choose to believe,' Caroline

snorted. 'But if you ask me you just don't know how to hold on to a man.'

'No one asked you, Caroline.' The day of reckoning had arrived between them, finally, as Robyn felt her temper tip over beyond the realms of control. 'And quite frankly I'm sick of your damned patronising,' she snapped. 'I work here, Caroline, I do not accept charity, which is more than can be said for you.'

'How dare you!' the younger woman gasped.

'Quite easily.' Her eyes flashed. 'I've put up with your rudeness and insinuations because of your father——'

'And because you would be out of a job otherwise!' Caroline scoffed.

'That's true,' Robyn acknowledged coldly. 'Why on earth your father loves a selfish little bitch like you is beyond me. But he does. So I'll save us all a lot of time and trouble and just resign.'

Caroline looked startled, her make-up livid against her sudden pallor. 'There's no need to do that——'

'It will save your father the embarrassment of asking me to leave.'

'He wouldn't do that,' Caroline flushed. 'He's more likely to ask *me* to leave.'

Her eyes widened. 'Don't be ridiculous——'

'It's true,' the younger woman flared. 'He admires you tremendously for the way you've coped with the twins since you've been on your own. He's always singing your praises,' she added resentfully.

And with surprised hindsight Robyn could see that a lot of Caroline's attitude towards her stemmed from the Colonel's admiration of her; she had the elderly man's respect in a way that

Caroline never could, and the younger woman was jealous of her. Amazing as that seemed, it was true!

'Caroline,' she began, thinking better of her gesture of friendship as she saw the other woman's expression tighten rebelliously. 'Would you mind taking over for me today?' she asked instead. 'I have some things I need to do.'

'I suppose I could,' Caroline said reluctantly. 'Does that mean you aren't leaving?'

She shook her head. 'I just need this time off to sort a few things out.'

'What things?' Caroline asked with avid interest.

'Personal things.'

The younger woman looked disappointed she wasn't to hear all the 'sordid details'. 'All right,' she agreed in a disgruntled voice. 'But only for this one day. I'm not paid to be the secretary around here,' she added with bitchy normality.

One day was all she needed. With Sin gone it was imperative that she talk to Brad and try to sort out what plans he had concerning the children. Once she knew that she could resign herself to whatever came next, either to fight him or continue her life quietly with the twins.

And once she had seen Brad she had to talk to Sin, had to make her peace with him.

'What are you doing?' Caroline watched with frowning eyes as Robyn leafed quickly through the Colonel's files. 'I thought you were leaving for the day?'

'I am.' She had finally found what she was looking for, making a mental note of Sin's London address. 'Right now,' she gave Caroline a bright, meaningless smile.

Her usual frugality when it came to petrol was forgotten as she drove herself up to London, too agitated by Sin's abrupt departure and her uncertainty about Brad's plans concerning the children to care about such things at the moment.

CHAPTER TEN

IT was too much to hope that Brad would be at home, although the call to his office she had forgotten to make before leaving home had him promising to be at his flat within the next half an hour.

'An emergency,' he said as he let them into his flat. 'What sort of emergency? Is it the twins? Come on, Robyn,' he encouraged impatiently. 'What's happened?'

She moistened dry lips. 'Are you going to marry Tina?'

'*That's* the emergency you dragged me away from a front-page story for?' he predictably exploded.

'Did you finish the story?'

'Yes,' he muttered grudgingly.

'I thought so,' she nodded.

'That's beside the point,' he flared. 'You deliberately made me think something had happened to Kim and Andy!'

'I didn't so much as mention their name,' she shook her head. 'And even if I had made the implication, it didn't exactly make you rush home,' she derided the time lapse between her call and his arrival here. 'Did it?'

He flushed at the taunt. 'I have a job to do.'

'So do I,' she said slowly. 'Are you going to let me continue to do it?'

Brad frowned at the question. 'How could I stop you working for Henry?'

She shook her head. 'That isn't the job I'm talking about.'

'Then what——'

'Brad, I won't let you take the twins from me,' she told him firmly. 'I'm their mother, they've lived with me all their lives, and what you're proposing is just cruelty.'

'What am I proposing?'

She flashed him a look of irritation. 'This isn't a game, Brad, this is something that could affect Kim and Andy for the rest of their lives.'

'What the hell are you talking about?' he made no effort to disguise his own irritation. 'I only had them to stay for the weekend, not did them some irreparable moral damage!'

'I'm not talking about the weekend——'

'Then what is it?' he demanded impatiently. 'You come up here in a panic, gibbering something about my ruining the twins' lives, and I have no idea what you mean. It's a little late to start issuing accusations for my feelings about your pregnancy five years ago, especially when I've tried to be the best father I know how to be. I should never have had children, we both know that,' he ground out.

'Then don't take them now!' she pleaded. 'Not just to impress your girlfriend.'

'Tina?' he frowned. 'What does she have to do with this?'

'You're going to marry her.'

He stiffened. 'Yes.'

'And so she'll become Kim and Andy's stepmother.'

'You needn't worry,' his mouth twisted. 'She won't try and interfere.'

'How can you say that?' Robyn gasped. 'Unless you intend getting a nanny for them?'

'For the twins?' he gave a bewildered frown. 'But I thought you liked looking after them yourself? You've certainly rammed your independence down my throat enough the last four years,' he grimaced.

'Brad, are you or are you not going to try for custody of the children when you marry Tina Fowler?' She was very tense as she waited for his answer.

'I'm *not*,' he spluttered disbelievingly. 'Most definitely not,' he repeated grimly.

Confusion darkened her eyes. 'Then why did you tell Sin that you were?'

Brad shook his head. 'I didn't.'

'But he said——'

'Yes?' Brad prompted interestedly, eyeing her speculatively as confusion washed over her.

What *had* Sin said exactly? Not that Brad had told him he wanted the children, only that *he* had told Brad they were getting married, to stop the other man making the claim. Now it seemed Brad hadn't been going to make it after all. How ironic that she and Sin should have argued about something that hadn't even been a possibility, if Brad's attitude were anything to go by.

'We both thought you wanted the twins,' she amended firmly. 'You've never had them for a weekend before.'

His gaze was suddenly evasive. 'No.'

'Brad?' she prompted softly.

He gave her a resentful glare, turning away abruptly. 'I'd been caught in a trap once before, I didn't intend for it to happen a second time,' he muttered in a barely audible voice.

Robyn tensed expectantly. 'Yes?'

He turned on her angrily. 'We can't all have

this paternal streak you revel in,' he bit out accusingly. 'Children just don't, and never have, entered into my plans. And so when Tina told me she didn't want children either I——' He broke off with a rueful sigh.

'Yes?' she prompted again, more warily this time, not liking where this was leading at all.

'Some women will tell you anything they think you want to hear,' he muttered. 'And then when you're well and truly trapped they do an about face.'

'I hope you aren't implying I did that?' she stiffened indignantly.

'No,' he sighed. 'We just didn't get around to discussing the fundamental requirements of our marriage until it was too late. With Tina I was taking no chances. I already have two children, I don't want any more,' he shook his head. 'This weekend was a test for Tina, to see if she really meant what she said,' he admitted reluctantly.

Robyn could hardly believe what she was hearing. 'You're saying you used the twins as *guinea pigs*?' she said with slow incredulity.

'It wasn't like that——'

'That's exactly how it was,' she stormed, her eyes blazing. 'Did your girlfriend pass the test?' she scorned with disgust.

'Robyn——'

'*Did she?*' she repeated with furious control.

'Yes,' he muttered.

'How?' she asked through gritted teeth.

'Robyn——'

'Will you just answer my question!'

He shrugged at her aggression. 'She was polite to them, even friendly, but it was obvious she wasn't comfortable with them. I asked her to marry me last night, and she agreed on condition I never ask her to cope with the twins like that again.'

'And you agreed to that?' she prompted in a hushed and disbelieving voice.

His expression was even more resentful. 'Yes.'

'You actually agreed not to have them stay with you ever again?'

'Yes!'

'You unfeeling bastard!'

'Now, Robyn——'

'The twins worship the ground you walk on,' she advanced on him angrily. 'And you *used* them in that cruel way, making them thoroughly miserable in the process. Oh yes,' she scorned at his surprised expression, 'they aren't just wooden objects to be pushed and shoved about, they were both very upset Sunday evening. That's how I found out about Tina Fowler; they didn't want to come and live with you either!'

'Then that's just as well, isn't it,' he bit out without regret. 'Because Tina and I will be moving to New York after the wedding; her father has offered me a top job on one of his newspapers over there.'

'You didn't waste any time,' Robyn said with distaste.

'Why should I?' he said resentfully. 'What's the point of marrying the boss's daughter if you can't take advantage of a little nepotism? And don't worry that my remarriage will affect you at all, the old boy would never see you homeless or jobless,' his mouth twisted.

'The Colonel?' she frowned.

'Mm,' Brad grimaced. 'At least my marriage to Tina means I don't have to try and keep in his good books any longer; Tina's father could buy him out several times over!'

Robyn was learning several unpleasant facts about her ex-husband this morning that she would rather have remained in ignorance of, being shown irrefutably that he was a self-centred bastard of a man. To use the twins in that despicable way——! And after the comments he had made lately about being the Colonel's only male heir she should have realised his feelings towards his uncle were purely mercenary.

'You sicken me, do you know that,' she grimaced her distaste, feeling as if she had a nasty taste in her mouth.

He gave her a pitying glance. 'And do you realise I don't give a damn what you think or feel,' he scorned. 'I've only kept up appearances with you and the twins for Henry's sake, once I'm in New York I can forget you even exist!'

'And the twins too?' she asked through stiff lips.

'I'll remember them at Christmas and birthdays, like other divorced fathers do. At least I'll only have to remember one birthday date,' he derided harshly.

She could accept everything but his deliberate disregard for two children who loved him very much, her hand coming up to catch him forcefully on the side of his face.

'You little bitch!' he sprang back, a hand up to his face. 'You caught my eye, damn you,' his expression was belligerent. 'It will probably be black and blue tomorrow,' he accused.

'Good,' she said with satisfaction, looking at him with dislike. 'Try explaining that to Tina!' She didn't wait for his reply but turned and walked out of the flat, moving with dignified calm.

She rested her head on the steering-wheel of her car once she got downstairs, waiting for the nausea to pass. Brad had to be the most despicable man alive, using everyone, even his children, as only a means to an end.

The way she felt right now the best thing she could do was go home and lick her wounds, feeling as if she had indeed been in a battle. But she owed it to Sin to let him know that everything was all right, that she was grateful for what he had tried to do for her, but it was unnecessary.

The address she had for him showed a block of flats very much like the one Brad's was in, although Sin had the penthouse apartment, the man behind the desk in the lobby asking for her name before calling up to Sin's apartment, allowing her to go up in the lift after a brief conversation with him. At least Sin hadn't refused to see her!

As she stepped out of the lift into the thickly carpeted hallway a woman was coming out of the door opposite, a tall glamorous blonde, her eyes wide as she spied Robyn, filled with a warmth that was intensified as she smiled.

'I'm Kay Thornton, Robyn,' she put out her delicate hand in a friendly gesture. 'As soon as you and Sin have sorted out this ridiculous mess you've made of everything perhaps you would like to come to dinner with Adair and me?' she invited brightly. 'And the children too, of course. My two will love meeting them.'

Robyn had eyes only for the man who had appeared in the doorway behind this beautiful butterfly of a woman, barely registering what was being said to her as she took in Sin's strained appearance, the tousled blond hair, the dullness of deep blue eyes, his clothes once again looking as if he had slept in them.

'Robyn?' Kay Thornton prompted softly.

'Er—Of course,' she dragged her gaze back to the other woman. 'Thank you.'

'That's perfectly all right,' Kay Thornton grinned. 'And I'll call you later in the week and tell you what you just agreed to,' she said knowingly before turning back to Sin. 'Call us as soon as you feel like being sociable.' She touched his arm gently before stepping into the lift Robyn had vacated and going down to the ground floor.

Sin looked at Robyn uncertainly. 'Would you like to come in?'

'Thank you.' She stepped past him, instantly liking the relaxed atmosphere the cream and gold decor aspired to, finding the lounge she had entered comfortable rather than ultra-modern, despite its size and obviously expensive furnishings. Sin liked to be surrounded by nice things, but he certainly wasn't obsessed with them.

'Is anything wrong?' Sin had followed her, standing dangerously close. 'Are Kim and Andy all right?' his voice sharpened with concern.

Her mouth twisted wryly. 'They're fine. And you're the second man to ask me about them today, but I have a feeling you really mean it.'

'Brad?' His eyes had narrowed.

'Yes,' she sighed. 'I—Would you mind if I sat down?' she looked at him appealingly, reaction setting in from the unpleasant scene she had had with Brad.

'As bad as that?' Sin frowned.

'Yes,' she confirmed huskily, sinking down into the soft brown chair.

She watched as Sin moved to pour her a brandy, not refusing it as she would have done normally, in need of something to steady her nerves. She also took the opportunity to look at Sin unobserved, struck by the difference in him in only a matter of the few days she had known him, the charming rake of their first meeting seeming to have gone for ever.

She sipped the brandy, feeling its warmth in her bones. 'I hope I didn't call at an inconvenient moment?'

'Kay?' his brows arched questioningly. 'She's my sister-in-law, remember?'

She did vaguely remember him mentioning the other woman. 'Adair is your brother?'

He nodded impatiently. 'You've seen Brad today?'

'Yes,' her voice shook slightly. 'You're right, he is going to marry Christina Fowler.'

'Oh.'

'But he doesn't want the children.'

'No?'

Sin didn't seem as surprised by this news as she had expected him to be, and she frowned her confusion. 'I just thought you would like to know.'

'Thanks,' he nodded, swallowing down some of his own brandy, grimacing slightly.

'Sin?' She was hurt by his lack of response.

He slammed the glass down with barely controlled force. 'What do you want from me?' he ground out, his eyes glittering dangerously. 'Congratulations? Commiserations? *What?*'

'Sin!'

He gave a heavy sigh at the pain in her voice. 'Why did you come here, Robyn?'

'I just told you——'

'I know what you told me!' His control snapped. 'But have you ever taken the trouble to listen to *anything* I've told you?'

'Sin?'

'Will you stop saying my name in that appealing way!' he groaned, his eyes closed. 'Don't you know yet what it does to me?'

She swallowed hard, not understanding him at all at the moment. 'Why are you so angry?' she asked in a pained voice.

'*Why?*' His eyes widened angrily. 'Because I've done everything I can think of but get down on my knees and tell you how I feel about you, and all you can do is throw my feelings back in my face! I *knew* Brad wouldn't want Kim and Andy if he married Tina——'

'How could you know that?' she gasped.

He grimaced. 'I knew Tina very well myself once.'

'Oh.'

His mouth quirked without humour. 'Her attitude towards children and animals disgusted me, she gave the impression both should be drowned at birth.'

'Then she and Brad make a good couple,' she said bitterly, remembering Brad's solution to her early pregnancy.

'Yes.'

'But I still don't understand why you would tell me Brad *would* want the children?'

He gave her an angrily impatient glance. 'Because I love you, you little idiot, and I thought then you would turn to me——'

'Don't call me an idiot!'

'No,' he sighed. 'I should be calling myself one. Because it made no difference, did it? I offered myself to you and all you could do was tell me you would rather lose Kim and Andy than marry me!'

'You didn't ever explain——'

'Explain what?' he rasped. 'I've loved you almost from the first moment I saw you, certainly from the moment you opened the door to me in cut-off denims and that provocative sun-top, and your two little replicas bounded down the stairs on that first evening. I looked at you and I loved you, and when you asked me later if I had any children I wanted Kim and Andy to be mine!'

'Not at the moment' he had said in answer to her question! 'Sin,' she said slowly. 'I've left one man walking around London with a black eye, and if you carry on the way you are you could be number two!'

His anger seemed to be in check for the moment. 'What did Brad do to deserve that?' he mused.

'I'll tell you that later,' she dismissed. 'First of all I want you to listen to me carefully. I—love—you. Did you get that, Mr Thornton? I—love——'

'I got it!' he ground out fiercely, pulling her into his arms. 'Did you mean it? You meant it,' he grinned ruefully as he just stopped her fist making contract with his face. 'Then why haven't you told me before now?'

'Why haven't *I*?' she gasped. 'You haven't exactly been shouting about your own feelings.'

'I've done everything else *but* shout them! The fact that I didn't just want a sexual affair with you should have told you how I felt. I even arranged with the Colonel for you to help with my research so that you would understand my work better——'

'And I do,' she told him hastily. 'I think your writing is wonderful.'

'Well at least that worked,' he grimaced. 'The trips I planned with the twins, designed to show you I intended being about for a long time to come, only resulted in my being accused of wanting to confuse Kim and Andy when they already had a part-time father! And I wanted to be a *full*-time one!'

'Well I wasn't to know that,' she protested indignantly.

'Because you wouldn't give me a chance—or yourself the opportunity to feel something for me. Even after we made love I tried to push you into admitting you cared for me; you just said you wanted an affair with me, one the twins wouldn't have to be aware of.'

'Sin, I had no idea you loved me!'

'Wasn't I obvious?' he said disgustedly.

'No,' she shrugged. 'Especially when the only reason you wanted to marry me was for the twins' sake.'

'I'd want to marry you if I had to crawl down the aisle with broken legs!'

'You never mentioned the subject of marriage until this situation with Brad arose!'

He scowled at her. 'A man needs a bit of encouragement, you know.'

'And going to bed with you wasn't encouragement?'

'Not when I wanted so much more than that!' Confusion suddenly flickered across his strong face as they glared furiously across the room at each other. 'Why are we arguing when we've just admitted how much we love each other?' he asked dazedly.

Her own anger began to fade, her breasts stopping their heaving up and down as her breathing began to steady. 'I don't know,' she finally grimaced. 'All I want to do is make love with you.'

'Kim and Andy?' he hesitated.

'I've arranged for them to go to a friend's house for tea; I had no idea how long I was going to be. I have to pick them up later.'

'Then we have all day,' Sin took her in his arms.

'How about a lifetime?'

'Does that mean you will marry me?' His gaze avidly searched her face as she looked up at him trustingly.

'If you won't mind being married to an idiot.' She smiled tremulously.

He kissed her gently. 'I'm sorry I called you that—even if you can be a little dense at times.'

This was more like the man she had first known. 'Did you tell your sister-in-law about me?'

He nodded. 'She knows me too well not to realise something was wrong when I stormed back to London this morning. But could we discuss our respective families a bit later?' he groaned raggedly. 'Right now I badly need to make love to you!'

'Please don't be angry, Sin,' she begged him as she lay beside him in the huge circular bed in his bedroom, leaning up on one elbow to look down at him, over two hours having elapsed before they felt in the mood to discuss their families, Sin absolutely furious about Brad's behaviour concerning Kim and Andy. 'He'll be going to New York soon, and now that he doesn't have to try and impress his uncle with what a loyal family man he is I doubt we'll see much more of him.'

'I'd like to black his other eye!' Sin stated grimly.

'It's over now, Sin, let's not spoil what we have.' She smiled. 'The twins are going to love having you as their father.'

'And I'm going to love taking on that role.' His smile was gentle. 'Am I allowed to take them on that skiing holiday now?' he teased.

She smiled. 'As long as I can come too!' She played with the softly curling hair on his chest. 'What was it you once accused me of wanting, "a no risk affair", wasn't it?' she mused.

He nodded. 'At the time it did seem to be all that you wanted.'

'Well,' her mouth quirked, 'it may have escaped your notice, Mr Thornton,' she teased, 'but we have taken several "risks" in the last few days.'

For a moment he looked stunned, then he grinned. 'So much for being a responsible adult. In that case there's something I think I should tell you.'

She sobered at his suddenly serious tone. 'Yes?'

'You remember I told you I'm the baby of my family?' he quirked blond brows.

She frowned. 'Yes.'

'Well it's true, I am,' he nodded. 'But only by about five minutes,' he admitted reluctantly.

Robyn looked down at him in stunned surprise for several seconds, blinking rapidly. 'You're a *twin*?' she finally managed to squeak. 'There are *two* of you?'

'Afraid so,' he grimaced. 'Although we aren't identical.'

'Thank God for that!'

'I'm the handsome one,' he claimed innocently.

'I'm sure Kay considers Adair is that!'

'Talking of Kay . . .'

'Yes?' she sighed. Surely he couldn't have any more surprises for her!

'She mentioned that she and Adair have two children . . .'

'They aren't twins too?' she croaked disbelievingly.

'Mm,' he nodded, looking at her appealingly.

'Oh God!' She fell back on her pillow, staring up at the ceiling.

Sin leant over her, gently caressing her cheek. 'Would you mind having my children?'

'I'll love it,' she answered truthfully. 'But the possibility of another set of twins is a bit of a shock,' she admitted ruefully.

'How do you think I felt the first time I saw Kim and Andy?' he derided. 'I knew my fate had been sealed from that moment on.'

'Poor Sin.' She touched the lean length of his jaw, loving him more than life itself.

'Lucky Sin,' he corrected with a groan as his mouth claimed hers once more.

Here's how to get this special offer from Harlequin!

AUGUST
TREASURY EDITION
COUPON

As simple as 1…2…3!

1. Each month, save one Treasury Edition coupon from your favorite Romance or Presents novel.
2. In four months you'll have saved four Treasury Edition coupons (<u>only one coupon per month allowed</u>).
3. Then all you have to do is fill out and return the order form provided, along with the four Treasury Edition coupons required and $1.00 for postage and handling.

EYE OF THE STORM

MAURA SEGER

A powerful portrayal of the events of World War II in the Pacific, *Eye of the Storm* is a riveting story of how love triumphs over hatred. In this, the first of a three-book chronicle, Army nurse Maggie Lawrence meets Marine Sgt. Anthony Gargano. Despite military regulations against fraternization, they resolve to face together whatever lies ahead.... Author Maura Seger, also known to her fans as Laurel Winslow, Sara Jennings, Anne MacNeil and Jenny Bates, was named 1984's Most Versatile Romance Author by *The Romantic Times*.

You're invited to accept 4 books and a surprise gift Free!

Acceptance Card

Mail to: **Harlequin Reader Service®**

In the U.S.
2504 West Southern Ave.
Tempe, AZ 85282

In Canada
P.O. Box 2800, Postal Station A
5170 Yonge Street
Willowdale, Ontario M2N 6J3

YES! Please send me 4 free Harlequin Presents® novels and my free surprise gift. Then send me 8 brand new novels every month as they come off the presses. Bill me at the low price of $1.75 each ($1.95 in Canada)— an 11% saving off the retail price. There are no shipping, handling or other hidden costs. There is no minimum number of books I must purchase. I can always return a shipment and cancel at any time. Even if I never buy another book from Harlequin, the 4 free novels and the surprise gift are mine to keep forever.

108 BPP-BPGE

Name _____ (PLEASE PRINT)

Address _____ Apt. No. _____

City _____ State/Prov. _____ Zip/Postal Code _____

This offer is limited to one order per household and not valid to present subscribers. Price is subject to change.   ACP-SUB-1

You're invited to accept 4 books and a surprise gift Free!

Acceptance Card

Mail to: Harlequin Reader Service®

In the U.S.
2504 West Southern Ave.
Tempe, AZ 85282

In Canada
P.O. Box 2800, Postal Station A
5170 Yonge Street
Willowdale, Ontario M2N 6J3

YES! Please send me 4 free Harlequin Romance® novels and my free surprise gift. Then send me 6 brand new novels every month as they come off the presses. Bill me at the low price of $1.65 each ($1.75 in Canada)—an 11% saving off the retail price. There are no shipping, handling or other hidden costs. There is no minimum number of books I must purchase. I can always return a shipment and cancel at any time. Even if I never buy another book from Harlequin, the 4 free novels and the surprise gift are mine to keep forever.   **116 BPR-BPGE**

_____
Name   (PLEASE PRINT)

_____
Address   Apt. No.

_____
City   State/Prov.   Zip/Postal Code

This offer is limited to one order per household and not valid to present subscribers. Price is subject to change.   **ACR-SUB-1**